Coke Kings 3

Lock Down Publications and Ca$h
Presents
Coke Kings 3
A Novel by *T.J. Edwards*

Lock Down Publications
P.O. Box 870494
Mesquite, Tx 75187

Visit our website @
www.lockdownpublications.com

Copyright 2019 T.J. Edwards
Coke Kings 3

First Edition September 2019
Printed in the United States of America

This is a work of fiction. Names, characters, places, and incidents either are products of the author's imagination or are used fictitiously. Any similarity to actual events or locales or persons, living or dead, is entirely coincidental.

Lock Down Publications
Like our page on Facebook: Lock Down Publications @
www.facebook.com/lockdownpublications.ldp
Cover design and layout by: **Dynasty Cover Me**
Book interior design by: **Shawn Walker**
Edited by: **Lashonda Johnson**

Stay Connected with Us!

Text **LOCKDOWN** to 22828 to stay up-to-date with new releases, sneak peaks, contests and more...

Thank you.

Submission Guideline.

Submit the first three chapters of your completed manuscript to <u>ldpsubmissions@gmail.com</u>, subject line: Your book's title. The manuscript must be in a .doc file and sent as an attachment. Document should be in Times New Roman, double spaced and in size 12 font. Also, provide your synopsis and full contact information. If sending multiple submissions, they must each be in a separate email.

Have a story but no way to send it electronically? You can still submit to LDP/Ca$h Presents. Send in the first three chapters, written or typed, of your completed manuscript to:

LDP: Submissions Dept
Po Box 870494
Mesquite, Tx 75187

DO NOT send original manuscript. Must be a duplicate.

Provide your synopsis and a cover letter containing your full contact information.

Thanks for considering LDP and Ca$h Presents.

T.J. Edwards

Chapter 1

Kammron scratched the back of his neck, with his eyes closed. He smacked his lips and took another line of the North Korean straight to the dome. "Yo', Kid, Shorty sound like she wil'in out. How the fuck she gon' be pregnant, then talking about she wanna leave?" He asked shaking his head.

Bonkers sat across the table from him with his hand on the handle of his Glock under his shirt. It was a week after Yasmin told him what she'd done regarding her and Kammron sleeping around behind his back. After he inquired further, she'd broke down and told him everything from beginning to end. Bonkers had been so heated, he had to stay holed up in a hotel for an entire week.

Bonkers eyed Kammron from across the table? "That shit do sound real fishy don't it?"

Kammron was high as heaven, his eyes drooped. "Yo', that's why I say the world is too big to be investing all your time and energy into one bitch. Word is bond, I don't give a fuck if she got a baby by me or not." He pulled his nose and smacked his lips loudly.

Bonkers felt his heart turning cold, as Jimmy walked into the room smoking on a Cuban cigar. He took a swallow from his orange and pineapple juice. "Yo', we gon' have plenty of time to talk about them hoes, B. Right now, we need to have a sit-down and talk about how we finna take over Queens, while at the same time keeping Harlem in check. It's a crazy world out there and them Vegas are only making shit crazier."

Bonkers waved Jimmy off. "Later for that bullshit, I need to holler at Kammron for a minute."

"What?" Jimmy asked, taken completely off guard.

Kammron was nodding in and out. He was so high he could hardly keep his eyes open. He tilted his head back and scratched his inner forearm again. "Kid, what you gotta holler at me about?"

"Why do you think, Yasmin, flexing on me when it comes to her pregnancy? You got something you wanna tell me?" he asked clutching the handle of his Glock even tighter.

Kammron smiled and ran his hand across his face. "Yo', why the fuck would I have anything to tell you, Dunn? You the one been running around trying to wife hoes and shit. It ain't got nothing to do wit' me." He opened his eyes and looked over at Bonkers.

Jimmy saw where this conversation was going. It was clear to him that Bonkers thought Kammron had something going on with Yasmin, and he was beating around the bush and afraid to ask him. He decided to cut to the chase. "Yo', Kammron, you got something going on with, Yasmin?"

Kammron snickered and pulled his nose. "I'm, Killa Kamm. The God ain't fuckin' wit' no bitch, life is too short for all of that being locked down shit. So, my answer is no." He closed his eyes for a second, then opened them back and looked Bonkers over.

Bonkers mugged him. "Kid, I been fuckin' wit' you ever since we been lil' project babies. I've always been one hunnit wit' you. I've always kept shit thorough, and I thought you was carrying on the same way. Nigga I need to know what happened between you and my bitch the night of the barbecue, the same night she went to pick up her laptop. She telling me one thing, but I need to hear what's really good from you. So, why don't you keep shit one hunnit and give me your side of things?"

Kammron laughed. "Nigga, you got the game fucked up. It ain't my bidness to get in y'all bidness. I don't know what, Shorty could possibly tell you about me because I don't fuck wit' her at all. I stay in my own lane; I got enough shit on my plate then to have to be worried about what you got going on wit' yo' bitch. That sucka for love shit ain't in me."

Bonkers clenched his jaw. "Nigga, I'ma ask you one time, did you force yourself on, Yasmin?" Bonkers took the gun out and sat it on the table. He'd already cocked it.

Kammron's eyes were opened wide. He mugged the gun on the table, and slowly trailed his eyes up to those of Bonkers. "Nigga, this what this shit is coming down too?" Kammron upped two pistols, and slammed them on the table, then pointed both barrels at Bonkers. His high dwindled just a tad.

Jimmy was shocked. "What the fuck y'all in here doing? I know you two lil' niggas ain't about to fall off over no bitch?" He looked from one young man to the other. He was shocked that things had gotten so far.

Bonkers curled his upper lip. "Nigga, did you force my bitch or not?"

Kammron ran his tongue across his teeth. "I ain't force your bitch to do shit. Nigga, I ain't even been wit' her under that context. I don't know why she lying on me, but once again I ain't got time to be worrying about another nigga's bitch. Life is too short."

Jimmy sat at the table. "Yo', are y'all kidding me, right now? You two are homies, n'all matter fact, y'all are brothers. I know damn well y'all ain't about to fall off over no female, especially when we just starting to get our money all the way up the way it's supposed to be."

Bonkers lowered his eyes and continued to mug Kammron. "Nigga, I love you. I'll die for you any second of the day. I care about you more than I do my own blood brother. I just need to know if you and shorty fucked around? If y'all did and that shit was mutual, I can deal wit' that. But if y'all did, and it wasn't then we finna have some major problems. Third to that if she lying, I gotta holla at this girl, because I know she don't like you, and if she's only saying this shit to drive a wedge between us I can't let that slide. I'ma have to handle my views accordingly. So, I'ma ask you one more time, bruh what was the real deal?"

Kammron was not finna let Yasmin divide them. He'd already had it in his mind he was going to get rid of her for the long run at his earliest convenience, but the first thing he needed to do was to fuck Bonkers' head up. After he accomplished that task, he would be free to go at Yasmin in the manner he needed to. "Yo', on all the love I have for you, Bonkers, and on my word to Kathy, I never fucked, Yasmin. I never would have," he lied. "If I even thought she would, I woulda told you, right away. You already know I ain't on that cuffing no bitch type shit, anyway. But me and her ain't even been alone before. I don't know why she kicking up this bullshit, but I'm ready to confront her in front of you. That's the only way you gon' find out who lying. Once you see I'm keeping shit one hunnit, you'll be able to make the right decision. But I'm letting you know right now that it ain't me."

Bonkers grabbed his gun from the table and stood up. "Nigga, we definitely gon do exactly that. I'ma sit both of y'all down tonight, and we gon get to the bottom of all of this."

Kammron kept his guns on the table and walked up to Bonkers. He held out his hand and gave him half of a hug. "Yo', it ain't nothing but love, Kid. Just another obstacle we gotta climb. In the end, I'ma be that nigga holding you down as usual. What time you trying to have this sit down?"

Bonkers rubbed his chin. "Shorty, get off work at eleven because she gotta go over a few things. She usually makes it home about fifteen minutes after eleven. We gon have that sit down right then. Gon' get to the bottom of all of this shit."

Kammron hugged him again. "That sound good to me, I'll make sure I be there."

Jimmy placed his hand on Bonkers' shoulder. "Now that y'all got this stuff figured out, for the most part, we need to focus on bigger and better things. Like getting money and staying rich. Bitches gon' come and go, but our love for one another has to be forever," Jimmy reminded them.

In to back of his mind, he was feeling some type of way about Bonkers saying he basically loved Kammron more than he did him, and they were blood. But it was a topic he would bring up at another time. At the moment he needed both men to be on their game. They had a huge task ahead of them, especially since talks with Tristan Vega had fallen through. Tristan had told Jimmy, Showbiz would stop at nothing until he'd broken Jimmy and all of Harlem down into pieces.

He told Jimmy Showbiz Vega was out for more than blood, he wanted to humiliate him, and anybody associated with him. Tristan thought war was bad for business, but Showbiz was dead set on wiping out Jimmy before he did anything else. Their father Chico Vega was dying swiftly, soon he would name a successor, and if it, was Showbiz that spelled lethal trouble for everything Jimmy had built. Tristan wanted Jimmy to come to some form of an understanding with Showbiz, but his hatred was just as bad, so there was no reasoning with either man. The only other option was war and murder.

"I'm taking a trip out to Jamaica so I can holler at, Flocka face to face. I'll be back in a few days, then we're going into overdrive. I need y'all to have ya game faces on. Either one of y'all got a problem with that?"

Bonkers shook his head. "I need to get my house in order. Once I find out what the deal is then I can move forward, but not until that time. It's as simple as that."

Kammron smiled sadistically. He already had smoking Yasmin on his mind. His plan was to get to her job first, so he could waste her before she had a chance to make it home. With her out of the picture, he and Bonkers could go back to the way things once were. The thought of Jazzy irritated him but not as much as Yasmin. He would take care of her later as well though? He'd already convinced himself of that.

"I feel the homie, and I can only imagine how much it's fuckin' wit' his mind. We gon' nip this shit in the bud tonight? Then we'll be able to go at the city of New York's throat."

Jimmy nodded. "Yeah, y'all get that shit under control so we can take over this—"

The front room window shattered, and a pepper bomb was tossed into it. Then another window shattered, and two smoke pepper bombs traveled through it as well. It was followed by a loud explosion before the rapid gunfire erupted. Jimmy's house filled with dark grey smoke and the trio found themselves under attack.

Kammron fell to the ground and pulled both of his weapons out of his waistband, as more shots were fired through the windows. The pepper smoke filled the living room choking him. His eyes became puffy and watery. His throat was scratchy, with every breath he took he felt like he was seconds away from losing a lung.

"Yo', Jimmy, I knew we shoulda wet that fool, Tristan. Look how they coming at us now!" He hollered before breaking into a violent fit of coughs. Snot ran out of his nose, and over his top lip. He fired toward the front of Jimmy's house. His bullets sailed out of the windows back to back.

Jimmy fell to his stomach, and low crawled across the floor toward his backroom that was equipped with heavy artillery. More slugs flew over his head and crashed into the walls of his hallway. His throat was so tight from the pepper bombs he struggled to breathe. When he made it inside of the back room, he flipped up the mattress from the bed and grabbed the M-90 from under it. He slammed a clip into it and cocked it. He fell backward into the wall, coughing into his inner forearm. His eyes were watering like crazy.

He slowly made his way out of the room, and to the back door, then he pulled it open and rushed down the stairs. He didn't know which of his many enemies it was currently attacking him, but one thing was for sure, he refused to roll over and play pussy. Jimmy was ready to give his enemies every slug inside of the magazine, even if it cost him his life trying to deliver. He opened the back door, and as soon as he was about to step into the back yard so he could run around to the front of the house and attack his adversaries from that vantage point, two of Showbiz's men were waiting for him. They kneeled on one knee with their full automatics and held their triggers as if their fingers had gotten stuck.

Boom! Boom! Boom! Boom! Boom!

The bullets chopped into the wooden door and knocked chunks from it. Splinters flew into the air, and in mere seconds the door was shredded by their artillery. They tossed another pepper bomb toward Jimmy. It exploded and blew him backward. His gun released from his hand and fell down the steps, on the fourth one it let off a shot. The bullet ricocheted and wound up punching Jimmy in the chest. He spun around and fell down the steps face first. He landed awkwardly in the basement, coughing, and hacking the whole way, as blood seeped from his wound thickly. He continued to cough and struggled to get up with no success.

Bonkers lay under the front room window looking for his opening to stand up and fire. Along with the thick cloud of smoke, there was also the rapid gunfire from Showbiz's troops. He had sent them on a mission of destruction, and they intended on destroying the Harlem natives by any means. Bonkers waited until there was a pause in the firing from his enemies before he jumped up, and began to spray his machine gun, finger fuckin' the trigger.

Blat! Blat! Blat! He fired.

His slugs slammed into their Excursion truck and rocked it from side to side. He continued to finger fuck his gat.

Blat! Blat! Blat! Blat!

"Muthafuckas!" he hollered standing tall. He watched the troops scatter for cover. They ran around the side of the truck and waited for him to pause in his gunning. Bonkers continued to buss until his gun jerked empty in his hand. Smoked drifted from the barrel.

From the gangway across the street, Showbiz zoomed into him through the scope of his military-issued Street Sweeper. He tapped the trigger, ignited the red beam. It landed on Bonkers' chest, then he was squeezing the trigger hard, over and over again.

The first bullet zipped from his barrel and traveled across the street. It punched into Bonkers' stomach and knocked him back just a tad before the second bullet hit his chest. Then the third his stomach, and the fourth another portion of his chest. He flew backward and fell into the glass table loudly. Showbiz took his eye off the scope and smiled under his Purge Mask.

Kammron saw Bonkers fall through the table. His eyes became bucked, even though they were leaking like a faucet. He struggled to his feet, rushed to his side, kneeled before him and placed his hand on Bonkers' chest, it was immediately covered in blood.

This made Kammron's heart skip a beat. "Aahh shit, Bonkers, hold on man! Aahhh, God please hold on!"

Kammron frowned and looked toward the window. He grabbed both Glocks and began firing in the direction of Showbiz's men as they were loading up to pull away from the street. His bullets tinged off the metal of their trucks. He continued to fire.

Blocka! Blocka! Blocka! Blocka!

The guns jumped in his hands, shells hopped from his toolies and rolled across the carpet. He stood right in front of the window, firing. "Aahhh, you bitch ass niggas! Y'all wanna fuck wit Harlem, huh?"

Blocka! Blocka! Blocka!

Bullets shattered two of the four trucks windshields before they sped off. There was only one truck left, and it was waiting for Showbiz.

Showbiz placed his eye back on the scope and zoomed the AR33 into Kammron. The plus sign on his scope lined up perfectly with Kammron's forehead. He smiled, with one squeeze of the trigger he could take Kammron's life away. He bit into his lower lip and placed his finger on the trigger.

Kammron emptied his clips and threw open the front door of the house in a drunken fury. He rushed onto the porch searching his waist for his 9mm. By the time he located it Showbiz's men were aiming their guns at him, ready to blow him from the face of the earth when Showbiz rushed from his vantage spot. He held his hand up, signaling for them to wait for his command. Kammron thought about upping his gun, but he was outgunned and outnumbered.

Showbiz rushed to him and raised the AR33. "Bitch, nigga if you move I'ma knock yo' head off and take that shit back to Brooklyn wit' me to gloat wit' my homies. Drop that mafucka, and we finna roll you around this block real quick. Hurry up before twelve pull up. Showbiz wasn't really worried about twelve showing up because he had already paid off the Jakes that patrolled that area. He had a five-minute window that he intended on using.

Kammron had visions of upping his gat and spraying, but it was a hundred percent chance he woulda been gunned down. He took a look back at Showbiz's house and saw the many bullet holes inside of it. He imagined it being him and swallowed his spit. His high wore off him almost immediately.

He mugged the masked Showbiz. "Fuck you wanna roll around the block with me for?"

Showbiz aimed his gun at Kammron's head. "This yo last warning. Drop that homeboy or we finna hit you wit' a hunnit shots like Dolph. Word to, Brooklyn."

Kammron mugged him for a second longer, before dropping his gun. "Come on, let's get this shit over with." Two of Showbiz's killas jumped out of their truck, and forced Kammron into the back of the excursion aggressively?

****

Jimmy slowly made his way up the stairs holding his chest. He'd already pulled the vest from his body and dropped it to the floor. He made it back upstairs, and into the house. There were still remnants of the pepper in the air that caused him to choke. He covered his mouth, as blood oozed through his fingers, dripping off his wrist. He struggled to breathe. He made it up and through the kitchen. He looked ahead, and saw Bonkers stand up, then fall right back down in the living room. His shirt was covered in blood. He'd fallen face first and began to shake.

Jimmy rushed to his side. The pain in his chest was momentarily forgotten about, as he slowly flipped him over. "Baby brother—baby brother! Fuck man, aww shit. Just hold on, hold on, please!" he hollered pulling out his cellphone calling for help. He felt sicker than a person with pneumonia. If Bonkers died, he would never forgive himself.

****

"That's it, pull over right there," Showbiz ordered his driver. The driver pulled over just at the edge of the rock quarry. Showbiz threw open the side door and yanked Kammron out of the truck. He flung him to the ground and upped his gun. "Now listen here homeboy I don't know what's really good wit' you, or how close you are to Jimmy? But it's a new day. All that shit he doing is about to cease to exist, and any mafucka rotating wit' him is about to feel the wrath of the Vegas. This here was just a warning to you Harlem niggas."

Kammron scooted backward on his ass. "Yo', fuck you, nigga. I don't know who you really are, and what you got against Harlem but pussy it's to the dirt wit' me if you think I'm finna ever ride against my homeland. Harlem run the world." The moonlight shined off Kammron's forehead.

Showbiz laughed. "Nigga, Harlem don't run shit. You niggas starving compared to what we seeing out in Brooklyn. As long as Jimmy is at the driver's seat, I'ma make sure you fuck niggas starve." Showbiz mugged him and cocked his hammer. He aimed the gun at Kammron's face. "Any last words, nigga?"

Kammron stood up with a scowl on his face. He staggered to his feet and edged closer to the edge of the cliff. He looked over it and felt like he had to shit. He swallowed his spit again. Then faced Showbiz, for him now wasn't the time to be hard and stupid. He had to use his street smarts. As much as he hated the sight of Showbiz's face, he had to play his role in order to stay alive. He held his hands open and held them at shoulder length. "Say, Dunn, if you wanted to kill me you would have done that shit back there. So, what's really good?" Showbiz sized him up. He was already prepared to splash him. He kept the mug on his face, extended his arm bringing the barrel closer to its mark of Kammron's forehead. "It's all about money for me. Right now, Harlem is standing in the way of the Vegas taking over New York, and thereby preventing the flow of nearly a half-billion dollars of assets a month. In addition to that, Jimmy is venturing out into Queens, a hot spot for the Vegas, and Vega Enterprises."

Kammron frowned. "Fuck that got to do wit' me?"

"You're in his circle, you're close enough. I'm looking for a man to replace, Jimmy. To keep his same plugs with, Flocka, and those Ponces' back on the island of Cuba. This replacement can be you, and if it is you should look forward to being a very rich man."

Kammron was appalled. "What you think I'm some turncoat or something?"

Showbiz shook his head slowly. "N'all, but I been watching you for a long time, Kammron. You're one of those flashy niggas. All about the money, glitz, glamour, and all that top-notch shit. Jimmy is out for self. He don't give a fuck about Harlem, never have, never will. But you bleed Black Heaven, you breathe Uptown. With you at the controls not only could you put your borough back on the map, you can get filthy rich while doing it. All you gotta do is fuck wit' me the long way." Showbiz smiled.

Kammron wanted to spit in his face. "And what happens if I decline?"

Showbiz knocked on the passenger door to the truck and was handed a book bag filled with two hundred thousand dollars in cash. "I don't think you wanna do that, Kammron. You and I both know you don't fuck with Jimmy like that. Besides, he don't give a fuck about you either. That's why he lives in a palace, and you stay in that second-rate apartment." He laughed he'd done his homework on Kammron. He knew Kammron was very prideful and held an utter disdain for Jimmy. He was working an angle he was sure to prove golden. He handed the book bag to Kammron. "This is two hundred gees, a gift from the Vegas."

Kammron unzipped the bag and looked inside it. All loyalty to Jimmy began to float out of the window. Kammron ran his hand through the money. The bills were crisp. "Kid, what the fuck you want me to do?"

Showbiz lowered his gun. "Come on, let's take a ride."

T.J. Edwards

Chapter 2

Three Weeks Later

Kammron stood over Bonkers' hospital bed with his hoodie pulled over his head. He took hold of his hand and squeezed it. Bonkers had so many machines, and monitors hooked up to him, it looked like the doctors were doing research on him. This was his third consecutive week in his coma, and there was no sign of him coming around. Kammron maintained a heavy heart.

He closed his eyes and shook his head. "Yo', how long the homie gotta be in this coma?" he asked Yasmin from across the bed.

Yasmin rested her hand on Bonkers' chest, then rubbed his face. "I don't know, but I just hope he comes around soon."

The monitors continued to beep in the background. She sighed, and had to fight back tears? Though Bonkers had only been in a coma for three weeks, to Yasmin it felt like an eternity. She felt so unprotected without him being conscious. Her heart could barely handle the thought of what could possibly take place for the worst. When she imagined life, she imagined Bonkers beside her at all times. She loved him like no other man that had ever been in existence.

She took a deep breath and rubbed his face again. "I still can't believe, y'all let this happen." She rested her head on Bonkers' shoulder.

Kammron dropped Bonkers' hand and stood back. He closed the hospital room door, and locked it, before walking back over to the bed? "Shorty, what the fuck you just say?"

Yasmin looked up and lowered her eyes. She frowned irritated. "Kammron, look, man, I already know you got a badass temper but now is not the time. I promise you that." She sat up and pulled the covers over Bonkers' chest. The sound of the breathing tube lodged down his throat was loud in the room.

Kammron walked around the bed and stood in front of her. "Bitch you acting like you ain't have shit to do with my mans making this stupid ass decision. All you've done since day one is feed that bullshit in his brain. This shit is just as much your fault as it is anybody else's." He ran his tongue across his teeth and looked her up and down with anger.

Yasmin stared up at him for a long time, then she hopped up into his face. "Kammron, any other day, I'd be scared of yo' ass. But at this moment my heart ain't pumping no Kool-Aid. Nigga, whatever you think you wanna do just do it. I swear to God, I'm ready. I'm sick of walking around on eggshells whenever I'm around you."

Kammron stepped in her face and clenched his jaw. "Aahh you tough now, huh?"

She looked into his eyes. "Never said I was tough, I'm just not in a mood to be afraid of you, right now. My man has been laying up in a hospital bed for three weeks now. The only thing I can think about and focus on is him. So, excuse me if I'm not spooked by you, right now." She rolled her eyes and looked back down at Bonkers turning her back to Kammron.

Kammron eyes trailed down to her ass. He relished in the sight of how her Prada sundress clung to her ass causing it to poke out. The dress was so tight he could literally see the crack of her valley. He bit into his bottom lip and groaned deep within his throat. He still couldn't believe how thick she had become. Not only that but her perfume was driving him crazy. Instead of retreating he took a step forward and placed his front on her backside. The softness of her caused his piece to rise.

Yasmin felt his piece and yelped. She tried to push away from him. "Kammron, get the fuck off me. What's your problem?" she asked angrily.

Kammron held her hips tight and grinded his front into her. "Bitch, I ain't tryna hear none of that shit. I'm tired of yo punk ass attitude. I'm finna give you something to be mad about." He pulled her dress up to her waist, exposing her pink thong underwear. He pulled her thong and rubbed his hand up and down her pussy lips, before yanking the crotch band to the side. Her dark-brown pussy was now on full display. The lips had hair on them because she hadn't shaved her sex since the last time she'd been physically intimate with Bonkers. The sight drove Kammron crazy. He forced her over Bonkers and stuffed his face in between her thighs from the back.

"Get off me! Please, Kammron, don't do this," she whimpered.

Kammron spread her ass cheeks and licked up and down her groove. Her saltiness added to his excitement. He sucked her pussy lips into his mouth, shivered, and slid his finger into her hole finding it hot, and snug. In a matter of seconds, his two fingers were a blur. He wanted to get that pussy nice and wet before he fucked her hard right while Bonkers was in the room. The taboo of it all was driving him insane. Kammron trapped her clitoris between his lips and sucked on it hard.

Yasmin moaned at the top of her lungs. She tightened Bonkers' sheet in her fists and tilted her head backward. "Stop Kammron, stop! Kammron, please don't do this. My man is right here!" she cried, once again trying to break free of his hold.

Kammron was too determined to allow her to be released. He licked in between her ass cheeks, sucked on her anus, and stood up unzipping his Gucci jeans. He pulled his dick through his boxer hole and placed the head in between her sex lips.

Her warmth surrounded him immediately. He eased forward and slammed home hard and deep into the recesses of her box.

"Aaahhh!" Yasmin closed her eyes and sucked hard on her bottom lip. "Get off me, Kammron!"

Kammron grabbed the back of her head and forced it into the bedsheets. He held her hip with one hand and fucked in and out of her at full speed. "Unnhhh-unnhhh-unnhhh. Shit Yasmin!" he growled, fucking her faster and faster. Her skin slapped against his. It sounded as if they were clapping hands. Her pussy got wetter. "Bitch you told—uh-uh-my nigga-uh-that—shit? That I—uhhhh, fuck!" He speeded up the pace. "That I took—this shit, anyway. So, I might—as well do it—" His dick ran in and out of her tight womb. It was leaking so bad her essence dripped off his balls.

Yasmin's face was turned sideways. She breathed heavy with her eyes closed. Her tongue traced her lips. She felt her ass jiggling and wanted to kill Kammron for treating her the way he was. She wondered what kind of a nigga would take his right-hand man's woman's pussy in the hospital room with his right-hand man in it? Kammron was a whole other kind of devil she saw. He yanked her backward, and fucked her harder and harder.

Kammron yanked her right arm out of its sleeve so he could play with her breasts. He found the nipple rock hard, and rubbery. He gripped the mound and squeezed it. It felt like a hot water balloon in his hand. His strokes were deep, searching for her bottom. "Call me, Daddy, bitch. Call me, Daddy!" He pulled her back to him faster and drove forward harder.

Yasmin began to make sounds she had never made before. Her mouth was open wide. She felt like he was in her stomach. His dick was too wide to deny its pleasure. Too long for her to ignore its enjoyment. Then the fact that he was circling her clit with his finger was enough to push her over the edge.

"Kammron—please, please," she moaned arching her back.

"Call me, Daddy, Yasmin! Tell me, I'm Daddy—tell me!" He slapped her juicy ass and watched the cheeks jiggle.

Yasmin yelped. "No-no—fuck you, Kammron! Fuck you—awww shit." She felt him pinch her clitoris again, and it was too much. She came hard, shaking all over Bonkers.

Kammron felt her pussy squeezing his dick, milking him. He pulled back, then slammed forward again, busting his nut deep in her womb. Then he pulled his dick out and picked her up from the bed. Instinctively, her thick thighs wrapped around him. He tossed her up and down, juicing her cat. Her essence dripped off his balls and oozed down his thighs.

He fell to the floor with her and forced her knees to her chest. "Bitch you gon' call me, Daddy. You gon' call me Daddy, right now." He started long stroking her so hard it became a long noise in the room. A steady slouching sound overtook those sounds of Bonkers' machines beeping and buzzing to keep him alive. "Call me, Daddy, Yasmin!" He slammed down hard.

Yasmin felt another orgasm rock thigh her body, and she wanted to kill Kammron worse than ever. She shook and moaned at the top of her lungs. "Aahhh, Daddy stop! Stop, Daddy—please! Uuuhhh-uunnhhh-unhhh, fuck—you're killing me!" One orgasm proceeded after the another.

Kammron bit into her neck and came hard in her pussy for the second time. He fucked forward and moved his body like a snake as he got the final remnants of his seed out of his body. When it was all said and done, he slowly pulled out of her and rubbed his dick head on her lips. "Come on, Shorty, clean me off—hurry up!"

Yasmin stared up at him with hatred. She grabbed a hold of his piece with her right hand and guided him into her mouth. She watched his reaction to her administering briefly before closing her eyes.

Kammron grabbed a handful of her hair and slowly fucked into her mouth until he came again? After he finished, he pulled out, and wiped his piece off with a wet wipe, and threw her the pack of them.

Yasmin smacked them to the floor. "Kammron, how could you do that? You already know I've been trying to be one hunnit to, Bonkers." She covered her face with her hands, and sat on the bed beside Bonkers?

Kammron dusted off his jeans and fixed the laces on his wheat-colored Timbs. "Yo, that ain't got shit to do wit' me. The way I see it, you was telling that nigga, I took your pussy anyway, might as well make that shit a reality. Besides, wit' him down for the count who you think finna be taking care of all of the bills?"

Yasmin uncovered her face. She couldn't believe Kammron had caused her to become unfaithful again. She felt sick to her stomach mostly because what they had done had been wrong, but there had actually been a sadistic part of her that enjoyed it.

She hated herself for admitting this. "Kammron, I don't need nobody taking care of me and Yazzy. I am woman enough to do that while my man is down. I don't need you to do nothing for me that I can do for myself. Word is bond."

Kammron waved her off. "I ain't tryna hear that shit. Far as I'm concerned, you're my responsibility, right now. So, in the name of the homie, I'ma make sure you and his daughter are good. Anything you need just holler at me, I'ma make that shit happen. That's my word." He fixed his Gucci belt and adjusted his fitted Yankees cap.

"Oh yeah, Kammron, and what am I going to owe you for doing that?" Yasmin asked dejectedly.

Kammron grabbed his Gucci leather off the couch in the hospital room and slid into it. A broad smile came across his face. "Shorty you ain't gotta do shit but give me some of this thick ass body when I need it." He pulled her up to him and wrapped his arms around her lower back.

She pushed at his chest and tried into wiggle free. "Let me go, Kammron. Let me the fuck go!"

Kammron tightened his hold. He looked into her eyes. "Shorty, you might be pregnant with my shorty, right now, am I right?"

Yasmin lost all fight, she trailed her eyes up to his. "Why are you asking me this, Kammron?"

Kammron trailed his hands down to her ass and cuffed it. "Because if that's the case that makes me and Bonkers damn near even. You need to honor me as an important nigga in yo life, Shorty. I'm finna take over New York all by my mutha-fuckin' self, mark those words? If you wanna be upgraded as a true Earth, then you'd jump on ship, right now? If not, I can leave yo ass standing somewhere."

Yasmin continued to peer into his eyes. She was so sick of being intimidated by Kammron. She wished there was some way to get rid of him for good. She was tired of him in more ways than one. "So, it's either I jump on deck with you, or you kill me?"

Kammron yanked up her dress and rubbed up and down her still leaking pussy. "Shorty, if I wanted you dead you'd be gone already. The way I see it you need me? Harlem got plenty of enemies. Once they catch wind that, Bonkers is down they gon' be looking to do something to you and your daughter. Mafuckas a do anything to clap back at us. Right now, I'm your first and last line of defense. It's time you respect a nigga." He eased two fingers into her pussy and pulled them back out.

Yasmin's eyes were closed when he pulled his fingers out, she opened her eyes. "You know what, Kammron you might be right. Look, I don't want to fight with you anymore. We both need to come together so we can support Bonkers during his time of need, and also so we can assure that both Yazzy and this unborn child is well protected." She placed her left hand on her stomach, and smiled weakly? She looked him over to see if the sight of her rubbing her stomach did anything to him emotionally.

Kammron wiped his fingers on a wet wipe. He noticed her nipples were rock hard. He wondered if she had truly enjoyed their sex act? He didn't know but if her wetness was any indication she had, then in his eyes she'd had a ball. "Look, Yasmin, you and I ain't gotta be the best of friends, but sooner or later you gon' fall in line. I like you so, that's just something you gon' have to deal with." He pulled her to him and kissed her neck. "I got you doe, Boo. I know you don't wanna hear that shit, but word to God, I do." He continued to rub all over her ass before he let her go.

He walked over to Bonkers, looked him over and shook his head. "It's fucked up what the homie going through, but life has to keep moving forward." He patted Bonkers on the chest, then looked up to her. "Until he wakes up it's you and I, Yasmin. That pussy belongs to me. That's just that, I'ma get at you later?" He kissed her on the cheek. She could smell the scent of her pussy on him, it caused her to cringe.

Yasmin watched him unlock the door, then he stepped out of it and was gone. She fell to her knees and broke into tears. Once again Kammron had caused her to cheat. Once again, he'd gotten the best of her. Once again, she hated herself for how she'd responded to the entire ordeal.

Chapter 3

Two weeks had passed and Bonkers was still in a coma, with no signs of him getting any better. Jimmy had told Kammron he needed to be out of the country for a few weeks so he could hobnob with Flocka out in Dubai. Before leaving he left Kammron with twenty bricks of North Korean and told him to do his thing.

Kammron wasted no time getting things in order. As soon as the weight was in his hands, he hit the ground running, and began to make drop-offs of large amounts all over Uptown. It seemed as soon as he dropped off a portion of the work to one side of Harlem, another side was calling him to pick up a substantial amount of cash. Things were rocking so good that was forced to call Jimmy in Dubai so he could re-up only a week after Jimmy had left. Because Jimmy was out of the country but didn't want to miss any money, he decided to give Kammron the low down on one of his many safe houses. It was something that Jimmy didn't want to do but under the circumstances, he really didn't have a choice.

A week after Kammron grabbed what he needed his cousin Duke rolled into town from Philadelphia. Duke was a dark-skinned, skinny nigga, with a bald head, and natural gray eyes that he'd inherited from his mother. He had a hot temper and was more trigger happy than most of the hittas in Harlem. He often referred to himself as 'Duke *Da God*'. He was born and raised in Harlem and had only moved out to Philly at the age of sixteen after he'd been charged with a double murder out in the Bronx while pulling a lick as a juvenile, even though he was acquitted of all charges.

Duke and Kammron stayed in contact, and after Bonkers went down he'd been the first person Kammron thought of as a replacement or temporary stand-in. He had mad love for, Duke Da God.

On the day Duke came to town, he rolled up on Kammron in a cherry red Jaguar, sitting on triple cheese Sprewell's. His windows were tinted black, and his car was knocking so hard that it caused the ground to vibrate. Kammron was just coming out of the house with Kammron Jr. in his arms when Duke stopped in front of the house. It was a bright, and sunny day. At seeing the car roll to the curb Kammron became on high alert. He pulled a .40 Glock from the small of his back and aimed ready to fire.

Duke smiled and lowered the passenger's window. "Yo', Kid, tuck that iron before I chop ya head off. What's really fuckin' good?" He asked throwing his hands in the sky-high enough to brush across the top of his car.

Kammron lowered his head and squinted his eyes. "Yo, don't tell me that's my muthafuckin' nigga, right there." Kammron became excited. He made his way down the steps of his stoop, and to Duke's whip.

Duke stepped out of the whip with the sunlight reflecting off his bald head. "Kid, what it do? I was gon' hit you up but I decided it'd be best if I just popped up on yo' ass. That way you can't be snubbing or ghosting a nigga, nah mean?" He gave Kammron a half hug and shook up with him.

Kammron took a step back and surveyed the atmosphere. He needed to make sure there weren't any enemies in sight. After confirming there wasn't he laughed off Duke's comments. "Nigga, you lucky you popped up when you did. I'ma about to take a drive with my lil mans, right here." He held up Kammron Jr. so Duke could see him.

Duke nodded. "Yo', Kid got your whole head already, Son. I'm talking your eyes and everything."

Kammron looked down on him proudly. "Yeah, I know, that DNA shit is crazy. Anyway, what brings you down to the Apple?"

Duke looked both ways, then curled his upper lip. "Got into wit' some fuck niggas back in Philly. A nigga needs a breather. I brought a lil' work wit' me and thought I could come over to Uptown and get some of it off. I already know you got this bitch lit."

Kammron couldn't help ceasing a moment to flex. "Nigga I am Harlem. I got this bitch hemmed up like a bully on a kid's ass at recess." He jacked and continued to bounce Jr. up and down.

Shana came out of the house with her Birken bag draped over her shoulder. She slid her Change sunglasses over her face and flipped her curly hair behind her back. She chirped her Mercedes Benz alarm and made her way down the stairs fitted in Chanel.

Duke's mouth dropped at the sight of Shana's thick ass. "Yo', who the fuck is that Earth right there, Kid?" He swore he'd never seen a female as fine as her in his life.

Kammron frowned and looked over his own shoulder. When his gaze fell upon Shana, he smacked his lips. "Mannn, the fuck out of here. That's who you talking about?"

Duke ignored him and brushed past Kammron. He blocked Shana's path and extended his hand. "How are you doing, Goddess? My name is Duke, you are gorgeous."

Shana blushed, she hadn't received a compliment from a man in so long it made her feel weird. She was afraid to extend her hand. Instead, she looked past her shoulder, and into Kammron's eyes.

Kammron stepped past them with a mug on his face. He handed her their son. "Where the fuck you think you finna go?"

Duke's eyes got bucked. He covered his mouth and sat on the hood of his Jaguar. The sun's rays reflected off his six gold ropes that were sprinkled with yellow diamonds. He had a huge piece decked out in crush white diamonds that read: *Da God.*

Shana took hold of Jr. and lowered her head. "I just wanna go get my nails, and toes done. I also have a hair appointment at two. I told you all of this yesterday." She was getting a tad irritated.

Kammron looked her up and down. He had to admit she looked good. She was rocking a pair of tan, red bottoms that set her outfit off. Her scent was alluring, and he could see what Duke saw from a physical standpoint. That irritated him.

"Yo', I don't give a fuck what you thought you was finna do on your own. Now you about to take my son wit' you. I gotta handle some urgent bidness." He didn't but he felt her having to carry their son around would cramp her style.

Shana was instantly devastated. She knew neither the nail shop or her beautician had a daycare space for Jr. If Kammron was going to spring their child off on her suddenly, then she was thinking she'd have to cancel her appointments until a later date. "Kammron, you know I can't take him with me to either of those places. He has to be with you for the day. At least until I can finish my tasks."

Kammron mugged her. "I don't care what you gotta do, but you gon' definitely take my son wit' you to do it. Like I said, I got some much-needed bidness I gotta take care of. If them bitches don't got nowhere for my son to be maybe we shouldn't be giving they ass bidness. You ever think about that shit?" He asked feeling a bead of sweat slide down the side of his forehead.

Shana could tell he was getting irritated. She didn't want to get into an argument with him. If worse came to worse she could find somebody to watch their son. The first person that came to mind was her mother Stacie. She was always down to watch him. The only problem with that was Kammron insisted that whenever Jr. wasn't with him that he be with her. That caused a massive strain on her social life.

She nodded her head in submission. "Okay, Kammron, that's cool. I got him, I'll he home around six or six-thirty. That cool wit' you?"

Kammron mugged her. "You muthafuckin' right it do. Don't be having my shorty out no later than that either."

Shana rolled her eyes and walked off. She couldn't stand Kammron at the moment. She simply wanted to get as far away from him as possible. "Yeah, well I'll see you tonight. Can you at least hold him while I run in the house and get his car seat?"

Kammron sucked his teeth. "Damn, why you ain't bring it out here wit' you?" He asked growing increasingly irritated. He nearly snatched their baby from her arms.

Shana stopped and took a deep breath. She smiled and looked toward the sky as if she was asking God for help. "Kammron, had I known you were going to pull this stunt, I wouldn't have made these appointments to begin with. I was unprepared. That's why I didn't have his car seat." She rolled her eyes again and headed for the stoop.

Kammron grabbed a handful of her hair and yanked her back to him. "Bitch, who da fuck you think you playing with, huh? You think you finna flex on me in front of my cousin because he thought yo' lil' popped ass was bad? Bitch please."

Shana yelped from the pain he caused her neck and scalp. She wrapped her hand around his hand and held it. "Kammron ain't nobody playin' wit' you. I'm sorry, damn, just let me go."

Kammron pulled her hair as hard as he could, then pushed her head forward. She stumbled on to the steps. "Bitch, just for that you ain't going no muthafuckin' where. Huh, take Jr. into the house." He handed her the baby and headed to Duke's Jaguar. "Yo', she might look good, but that bitch is a head case Son, word up. Let's get the fuck out of here so we can talk bidness and strategy."

Duke nodded and watched Shana walk up the steps with tears in her eyes. He felt some type of way for her even though he didn't know her. He couldn't help but notice the way the jeans molded to her ass and caused her cheeks to look so heavenly rounded. He couldn't believe how fine Shana was and hated the fact she had a baby by Kammron. He knew it was going to be hard to get her out of his mind.

****

Flocka slid Jimmy the golden platter laced with pure North Korean across the table. Jimmy took his razor blade and chopped through it, before creating two thin lines. After the lines were created, he took them one at a time, and fell back in the big wicker chair, while two bronzed East Indian women stood on either side of him with a big leaf fanning both he and Flocka. Flocka had two women on each side of him doing the same thing. Jimmy was faded, it felt like the world was moving in slow motion.

Flocka pulled on his nose and cleared his throat. "So, ya telling me in order for things to flow properly ya going to need more security, and more assassins to go at these Vega boys? Seems the Bombaclat Showbiz has a vendetta against you that can only be sealed in blood. If dats the way he wants to play tings Mon, den it's only right we gigging him the issues he's searching for." Flocka picked up the golden chalice that was filled with Red Wine. He swished it around in his mouth and swallowed.

Jimmy scratched his arm with his eyes barely opened. The raw coursed through him and numbed his entire body. He heard the bells sounding. It seemed as if Flocka sat across from him moving I'm slow motion. He struggled to open his eyes. "Fuck, Showbiz Vega. I been banging that fuck nigga since Havana. Now that he got a lil' prestige from his father he thinks he ready to fuck in my bidness. Truth be told I shoulda whacked his punk ass a long time ago. That fool ain't nothing but—" His eyes closed, he dozed off for a second, actually started to snore.

Flocka laughed from the other side of the table. He knew they were fuckin' with some good dope. It came imported directly from North Korea untouched. Each package had tiny pictures of Kim Jung Un on them. He bought them for ten thousand euros apiece and flipped them for sixty gees a whop. He needed to conquer at the very least two Burroughs of New York? He already had Harlem, and there was no way he was about to allow Queens to slip out of his hands. He would waste no time giving Jimmy the security and personnel he needed. Besides he could sit back and watch everything unfold from a distance. When you had large amounts of money you were always able to maintain puppets. To him, Jimmy was nothing more than that. He slapped his hand on the table loudly.

Jimmy jerked awake and wiped slob from his mouth. He pulled on his nose. His entire body was vibrating. "Yeah, yeah, yeah, Flocka. We gotta move them Vega boys around man. Queens is for the taking. Harlem is already ours. We're close to making a million dollars a day." Jimmy's eyes got heavy again. His eyes rolled into the back of his head for a second. He smiled and hugged himself. Then he was snoring loudly.

Flocka picked up the golden Chalice. "Ladies this is what takes place when you're not a King. Look at him, what filth."

He felt grossed out watching Jimmy drool at the mouth. The girls smiled at him and continued to fan both men. Jimmy began to snore so loud it got irritating. Flocka continued to look him over in distaste, shaking his head.

Chapter 4

There were three knocks at the door. Yasmin placed her phone on the table and got up. She'd been reading a book by Jelissa called '*Love Me Even When It Hurts*,' and for two entire hours she'd remained spellbound, it had been the only thing that helped her keep her mind from dwelling on Bonkers' condition. Behind her, the fireplace roared like a mini bonfire. *Sadé* played softly in the background. She had an incense burning that sent the scent of Myrrh into the house. It made her feel at peace. Before stepping to the door, she pulled back the curtain and peeked out the window. As soon as she saw Kammron she felt a chill go down her spine? They locked eyes.

She closed the curtain. "What's good, Kammron?"

"Yo,' open the door, I need to holla at you for a minute." Kammron pulled the Prada hood over his head as the wind coursed across his back. It was eleven o'clock at night, and he was lifted. He'd just left a strip club with Duke and was feeling some type of way.

Yasmin placed her back against the door and sighed. "Kammron, it is eleven at night. There ain't nothing we need to talk about this late that we couldn't have talked about on the phone. Go home, I'm in bed, and so is, Yazzy."

Kammron mugged the door. "Shorty, man, on everything don't play wit' me. Open this mafuckin' door." He took a sip from the bottle of Patron and wiped his mouth with the back of his hand.

Yasmin was caught in a dilemma, she knew Kammron couldn't have had anything positive on his mind, and if she opened the door for him more than likely they would wind up in bed together with or without her consent. She felt she had already crossed Bonkers enough. Her conscious was eating away at her. On the flip side, if she didn't answer the door, she didn't know what Kammron would possibly do. He was a loose cannon and could be very petty. Since Bonkers was out of commission, she had no one to protect her from Kammron, she found herself in a bind. It was either submit to his will or face the consequence that coulda been anything.

"Yasmin, if I have to say this shit again word is bond, I'm finna kick this mafuckin' door in!" he shouted with growing irritation.

Yasmin sighed and reluctantly turned the lock on the door. She pulled it open and stepped to the side with her head down. "Come in Kammron but be cool so you don't wake up, Yazzy."

Kammron staggered on his feet and waved her off. "Girl, ain't nobody finna wake her up?" He stepped past her, and into the front room. Then kicked his shoes off, and made his way to the couch, with the bottle of Patron in his hand.

Yasmin kept her head down, and closed the front door, locking it. She took a deep breath and turned to face Kammron. She exhaled and made her way to the couch sitting across from him. "So, Kammron, how may I help you?"

Kammron squinted his eyes at her. "Yo', you wanna know what's really starting to piss me off?" he asked scooting to the edge of the sofa, setting his bottle of liquor on the table.

Yasmin looked up at him, and once again sighed. "What's that, Kammron?"

He frowned. "Yo', you be acting like it ain't my right to come over here and see you whenever I feel like it. You got my muthafuckin' baby inside you. You ain't got no ring on your finger, and the way I see it, you're just as much my woman as you, is that nigga's."

Yasmin stood up. "Whoa, whoa, whoa, now. Kammron, you talking about Bonkers as of, he's one of your enemies or something. You guys have always been real cool. If anybody supposed to be holding him down, it's supposed to be you." She ran her fingers through her curly hair.

Kammron smacked his lips. "Man miss me with all of that bullshit. That is my nigga. And always will be until the death of me. Don't try and make it seem like I'm shitting on him or something because I'm not. I'm just stating the obvious. I got just as much claim to you as he do, point blank period." He took another swig from the bottle and stood up. He set it back on the table and made his way to her.

Yasmin held her arms out stopping him. "You got shit real twisted, Kammron. I never told you I had your baby. I said that because you and I wound up getting down around the time I got pregnant, there was a possibility you could be the father, but nothing is set in stone."

Kammron wasn't trying to hear none of that. He couldn't understand why but Yasmin had been doing things to his mind he couldn't quite comprehend. Every time he thought about her now it caused his manhood to stir. She made him yearn for her without actually pursuing or seducing him. Kammron took a step forward and grabbed her around the waist. He pulled her to his body and inhaled her scent. Her body felt hot against his. She was so small compared to him, thick in all the right places, yet so delicate.

He peered into her eyes, and got weak, with an overwhelming sense of possession. "Yasmin, I don't give a fuck about none of that. Until we find out what's really good, and until Bonkers wake up, you belong to me. I just gotta have you, and I'll smoke something over you, Goddess, word to Kathy in heaven." He trailed his hands down and cuffed her ass cheeks. Then placed his face within her neck and inhaled her scent.

Yasmin closed her eyes, she could smell the liquor on him. The smell of it threw her off. "Kammron, I know you're drunk, and you're feeling some type of way, but this ain't finna happen tonight. You need to leave, I gotta get up early in the morning, and accompany Yazzy on her field trip. Then I have to meet with a few investors that are going to help me take our beauty salons to the next level. By the time Bonkers come out of that coma he needs to see that I've been handling my business and taking our family to the next level."

Kammron's hands had been moving all over her ass, but at the mentioning of her and Bonkers having a family together, it instantly got him irritated. He pushed her back, and she fell on the couch. He placed his hands on his hip and looked down at her. "Shorty, you be blowing with the shit you be saying out of your mouth. When you gon' start referring to you and I being a family, especially if that baby turns out to be mine?"

Yasmin lowered her head, she felt anger rising. She needed him out of their home before she said something she regretted. Deep down she was tired of being bullied by Kammron. She couldn't wait until Bonkers woke up out of his coma so she could tell him how Kammron had been acting toward her. As much as she wanted to keep the drama down, she felt she had to let Bonkers know what was going on because more than anything it had to stop.

Kammron kneeled beside her. "Answer me, Shorty," he said through clenched teeth. From this level the scent of her perfume became heavy.

"Kammron, it will never be me and you. We will never be a family. I love Bonkers, and I always will. Now can you please leave?" She insisted, ready to stand up.

Kammron held her down by her thighs and mugged the floor. "You just gon' keep tryna treat me right. That's the bullshit you on?" He squeezed her thighs unbeknownst to himself.

Yasmin felt the pain and winced. "I'm not trying to treat you, Kammron. I'm just telling you how I feel. I can't help how I am feeling, right now, please just—"

Kammron was on his knees. He yanked her short nightgown all the way up her thighs, exposing her light blue Victoria Secrets thong. His face was between her thighs, sniffing the crotch. The aroma of her perfumed pussy sent him into a frenzy. He kissed all over it, then licked up and down the material.

"I gotta have you, Yasmin. I just gotta have you whenever I want you. Fuck the homie, right now, it's about you and me." He pulled her band aside, exposing her naked sex. He kissed her right on her juicy lips, opened it and licked up her dew. The first taste of salt caused him to shiver uncontrollably.

Yasmin held the arms of the sofa. She threw her head back, and closed her eyes tighter, as she felt his tongue penetrate her groove. Then it was tracing circles around her pearl. Tingles rumbled through her, and the next thing she knew she was moaning angrily. As irritated as she was her body acted as if it didn't understand she didn't want it. In a matter of seconds, she was spewing her essence over her sex lips, and on his tongue.

Kammron felt her jerk, and it excited him. He clutched her thick thigh tighter and pulled her to his face. Then he was going to town loudly, licking, sucking, and slurping her juices. He was hungry for them, excitedly searching for every pinch of them. He held her lips wide open exposing her pearl and trapped her clitoris between his lips suckling on it.

Yasmin arched her back and wrapped her thighs around his neck. She couldn't help moaning again. She humped into his face, and rode it, hating herself for doing so. When a strong current shocked through her and turned into an orgasm, she took a pillow off the couch and screamed into it as loud as she could. Kammron's fingers running in and out of her was too much. She popped her thighs wide open and came a second time.

Kammron continued to suck all over her pussy? He stood up stroking his unleashed penis. The head was as big as a crab apple. "I gotta have some of you, Yasmin. You're my ma-fuckin' woman now. I need some of that pussy, now! Bend that ass over this sofa. Come on, let me fuck you in y'all living room, and turn you into my, Bitch."

Yasmin stood up on wobbly legs, she held her hands out at arms-length, and slowly shook her head. "Not tonight, Kammron. Yazzy is in the other room, she could come in here in any second. I can't risk it, besides that, we can't keep doing this too, Bonkers. Sooner or later one or the both of us is going to have to show him some loyalty."

Kammron turned her around and bent her over the couch. He pulled her gown all the way up her hips and kicked her legs apart. Once they were apart, he took his piece and forced the tip between her sex lips, as he held her hips and slammed her forward.

"Awww, shit!" Yasmin's groaned.

"You think I give a fuck about being loyal to, Bonkers? That's my nigga, but I'm taking care of shit, right now. I'm sitting all alone. You're, my bitch, that nigga sleeping." He began to long stroke her at full speed, diving deeper and deeper. Her ass clapped back into him over and over, jiggling. The feel of her flesh was driving him insane. He squeezed her booty and slapped her ass cheeks hard.

She yelped and dug her nails into the pillows of the couch. "Aaahhh-aahhh-aahhh-aahhh, Kammron, please! Un-hhh-uunhhh-unnhhh-unhhhh-unhhh, Kammron! You're—aaahhh—"

Kammron clenched his teeth and held onto her hips fucking her as hard as he could. As usual, she got wetter and wetter until she was drooling from her cat. The feel of it only excited him further. "Aahhh, Yasmin." They continued fucking, and Kammron started long stroking her as their skins clapped together. "This my pussy now-this my pussy—it's mine! Aaahhh-I'ma-fuck-it-whenever—aaahhh—whenever— uhhhh—I wanna hit this shit!" He was fucking her so fast and hard slob dripped down the side of his face. Yasmin's ass was a blur in his lap. Her pussy began to make all sorts of noises that encouraged him to go harder.

Yasmin had tears running from her eyes as the orgasm rocked her body. She gripped his piece with her walls, and came all over his dick, inadvertently bouncing back into his lap again and again. She went putty in the knees and buckled.

Kammron picked her back up and continued to fuck. When he looked down at her caramel ass and saw the way the cheeks wobbled and shook it pushed him over the edge. He dug his fingers into her sides, and came spurt after spurt, jerking against her.

Yasmin felt his splashes and came again as the hot jets tapped the insides of her womb's walls. He pulled out of her and continued to shoot all over her ass. The droplets made her feel dirty and used. She sank to the carpet on her side, curled into a ball and sucked her thumb as more tears poured from her eyes.

Kammron stood over her, his piece still jumping, and shiny from her secretions. "Yo', Yasmin, get up ma," he ordered feeling some type of way.

"Just leave me alone, Kammron. You got what you wanted. Now just leave me alone." She closed her eyes and began sobbing.

Kammron frowned down at her. He felt emotionally attached to her and didn't like the feeling. He was used to smashing females and keeping it moving. The last thing he wanted to develop was feelings for anybody outside of himself, especially after losing his mother Kathy. Feelings he felt only set him up in a vulnerable position to be hurt.

"Just go away, Kammron, I can't believe you did this to me again." She shook her head. "I don't know how much more of this I can take." Her sobbing intensified, she felt so weak and lost, she hated the feeling. Whenever Kammron was around, he made her feel lower than scum, and less of a woman.

Kammron sighed and clutched his piece. He kneeled down and rubbed her side. "Yo', Yasmin, stop crying, Ma, I'm sorry." His eyes drank in her body, her nipples were still erect, and the sight of them did something to him.

"No, you're not, Kammron, all you care about is you. You don't give a fuck about nobody but yourself. Please leave my house. Just go, I need to be alone." More sobbing ensued.

Kammron kneeled for a hot second, looking her over. He didn't know what to do. Didn't know how to deal with the emotions and feelings he was experiencing for her. "Yo', all I can say is, I'm seriously sorry, and I do care about your feelings. I didn't mean to do this. I don't know how I've become so addicted to you, but I have. Don't worry, I'ma break up out of this shit you can believe that." He leaned down and kissed her soft cheek. It felt hot to him, once again her scent caused him to shiver.

Yazzy tiptoed down the hallway until she was standing in the doorway of the front room. "Mama, can you come to bed wit' me? I'm scared and I miss, my daddy."

Yasmin jumped up and wiped her tears away with her back to Yazzy. She swallowed the lump in her throat and took a deep breath, then gazed over at Kammron. "Please leave, Kammron. I need to take care of my daughter."

Kammron got dressed and pulled ten thousand dollars in all hundreds from his right front pocket. "Yo', I bought this cash over here for you. It's ten gees, and you can do whatever you wanna do with it." He held it out to her.

Yasmin shook her head. "I'm okay, Kammron. Our business is still doing really well. I'm meeting with a few investors tomorrow. I'll be okay, just leave, please!" She waltzed to the door and opened it for him.

Kammron shrugged and stepped through it. "A'ight, fuck it den. I ain't finna force you to take my money. But one of these days you gon' need me, and you gon' quit treating me like one of these other fuck niggas." He yanked her to him and kissed her lips, then licked them, and pushed her back. Over her shoulder he could see Yazzy standing behind Yasmin with her mouth covered by her hands, then he was gone.

T.J. Edwards

Chapter 5

Duke '*Da God*', sent one last lick up and down his Dutch before he set fire to it. In a matter of seconds, the Ganja drifted into the air. He took five deep pulls and inhaled hard, as the motorboat danced up and down on the waves of the water. The sun shined bright in the sky, there was a light wind coming from the north side of the harbor.

Kammron kept the duffle bag filled with seven hundred thousand dollars in cash on his lap. It had been an entire week since he'd saw or spoken with Yasmin, but she continued to dominate his thoughts. He hated himself for thinking about her so much. There were so many bad bitches in the world, so many that was crushing her, and in his heart, he felt he could have them all. Instead of him being preoccupied with thoughts of them, all he could think about was her.

Duke blew the smoke into the air and looked back at Kammron. He could see that he was lost in deep thought. "Yo', Kid, word is bond, you finna have to snap out of that bullshit. We about to meet up with these crazy-ass Vega niggas. Now I don't give a fuck what they telling you, or how one hunnit they're swearing they are. They got a reputation for being cutthroats. I don't know why you wanna lay in bed wit' these niggas to begin with? From what I see you been making money wit', Jimmy?"

Kammron clutched the Tech-9 in his right hand and peered over the murky gray waters. The smell of dead fish resonated in the air. He stood up and sat the duffle bag back on the chair. "Like I said, fuck that fool, Jimmy. That nigga is already rich. He already got his palace, it's time we get ours? Ever since them Jamaicans been up here following him around. He been doing his own thing and recruiting niggas out of Harlem so they can fall under his Byrd gang."

"Byrd gang?" Duke questioned. "What the fuck is that?" He cruised through the waters and checked his GPS system. They were ten minutes out from the spot they were set to meet Showbiz, and Tristan Vega, right on the shoreline of Havana, Cuba.

"Jimmy been hollering that Byrd gang shit ever since we were kids, but ain't nobody bites it. I guess since he got a nice amount of money, and Jamaicans backing that, he's in the perfect position to form what he always wanted." Kammron shrugged his shoulders. "I don't know, but I for damn sure ain't falling under him or no man. Word is bond, Kid, I go where the fuck I wanna go and do what the fuck I wanna do. It's the only way a man can get rich nowadays. Jimmy saying a mafucka can't even push these pieces in Harlem if they ain't fuckin wit' his Byrd Gang. I ain't tryna hear none of that."

Duke laughed. "Kammron, you stay pushing it to the limit. For as long as I've known you, you've always gone against the grain. I like that self-made shit."

"Not just self-made Duke, I'm a born diplomat, Kid, word to Kathy. Diplomats do what the fuck they wanna do. They go where they wanna go, and they set up shop on other people's shit. Anything go wrong they holla Diplomatic immunity and beat them cases. I just copped Kamina, too. I don't know when I'ma need him, but I definitely dropped a hundred bands into his lap for the future." Kamina was one of the best lawyers in all of New York. He specialized in criminal law. Kammron felt safe with the insurance Kamina bought him.

Duke nodded. "That what's up. I still say we hustle hard for a few seasons, then link up wit' Flame 'nem. Kid just bought this lil' label. He got a bunch of hot artists that's attacking them charts. They doing everything from singing to rapping, it's clean money, and that shit a last longer than whatever the fuck we out here doing. Besides you still spit them bars, right?"

Kammron laughed and thought back to when they used to stand in a cipher in the middle of Ruckers Park freestyling for hours at a time, high as a kite. Kammron hadn't got down in years, but he still had bars like a jail cell. "You already know I got that piff."

"Word to Harlem, Kamm, I'm high as a muthafuckin' kite. We about ten minutes from the meeting spot. Why don't you lace the Kid wit' a few bars?"

Kammron sat down and pulled the duffle bag to his lap. The North Korean had him feeling breezy. The last thing on his kind was rapping, he didn't feel like doing it, but it could help him get Yasmin off his brain. He figured why not?

"Fuck it, I think I got a freestyle in me, check it." He nodded his head and caught a beat in his mind. "A'ight, here it go. Word to Harlem, yo, yo, ay man fuck you faggots, either you ride wit' Kamm—or sleep wit' maggots. My whole life I been sworn in it—bring heat and on the chief, you pussies get tormented. Bring ya moms in it cause we playing or blood, the beam aimed at ya skull, den empty a dub. Whether it's night or the daytime, it's the right time, kids jumping rope in the streets, we still pop nines. Fuck using gloves or masks, this Harlem, we walk up in Gucci suits and tuxes disguised as Pastors.

"Who want heat wit' the Diplomat? I'm radical drop bombs and watch ya throat piece swell up the lawns. From Harlem to Illinois, niggas kill that noise, the God bring flame that a scorch you, boys. Prada purses for the Earths that a set you up. New Benzes for the Gods that a wet you up. Heavy bling, watch the Dunn flex, and my ding-a-ling—swing!" He started laughing and opened his eyes. "Yo', that's just off the top of the head? I got sauce though, we can fuck wit' that nigga, Flame when the time is right, for now, we need to focus on this move right here."

Duke smiled. "Yo', you got crazy talent, Kid. One day you gon' take heed to ya blessings and leave this street life behind. Word up."

Kammron sniffed and pulled his nose. "Yeah, one of these days."

****

Showbiz mugged Kammron from across the pool and took another shot of Patron. He tightened his Gucci robe around him and slipped his feet back into his slippers. He had a 9mm tucked into his waistband. He grabbed his drink and made his way around the deck toward the young Savage that he could already tell he wasn't going to allow to live long. He found Kammron to be too cocky, too outspoken, and a bit of a loose cannon. All of the characteristics that were himself. That irritated him because he felt there was only enough room in the world for one of him. But he had to be smart. He needed Kammron in order to get closer to Jimmy. Now that Jimmy was getting financial backing and security from the Jamaicans it made it harder to vanquish the Harlem native, although things went deeper than Harlem. They transferred all the way back to Havana where he and Kammron currently were.

Kammron stepped out of the pool, his Polo boxers clung to him and outlined his dick print. He fixed his shorts and brushed the water off his waves. There were so many thick, fully naked, Cuban women around the pool he could barely think straight. Every time he thought he saw one that was the baddest woman he'd ever seen in his life, another one popped up physically murdering the last. Kammron extended his hand, and they shook it.

"Yo', Showbiz, these bitches fine as a muthafucka, Kid. My words Havana got shit on lock." Showbiz played it off as if it was nothing. "Yo', this is an everyday thing, you'll get used to it." Kammron continued to look around, his eyes landed on two Cuban females with long flowing hair, as they hugged one another, and started kissing passionately while their hands roamed all over each other's bodies. When one of their fingers entered the other's twat, Kammron couldn't help but smile and becoming transfixed with the action.

Tristan walked up from behind him and laid his hand on Kammron's shoulder. "My friend, it's so nice to see you again. How was the boat ride, any problems from Customs?"

Kammron brushed his hand off his shoulder? He really didn't like niggas touching him and shit. Across the way, Duke kept his hand close to his waistband ready to up and splash anything moving? He didn't trust the Vegas and thought Kammron getting into bed wit' them was the wrong idea. He counted the ten bodyguards the Vegas had roaming around and figured if it came down to it, he would be able to hit each and every one of them.

Tristan cringed, and wanted to say something to Kammron about brushing off his hand but decided against it. Instead, he waited for him to respond. The sun beamed off his handsome face. His gray eyes were tuned into Kammron. "Well?"

Kammron shook his head. "They musta recognized the boat cause they ain't fuck wit' us. I got something for y'all." He grabbed the duffle bag from the side of Duke's foot and handed it to Tristan. "That's seven hundred thousand dollars right there. It took me three nights to make it, and that's with Jimmy basically conquering Harlem. I got a few buildings now, and I need a heavier plug, fuck this light-weight shit that y'all been dropping off? I can get these type of crumbs from,

Jimmy." He snatched the Moët off the table and turned up the bottle.

Showbiz mugged Tristan. He thought Kammron was very disrespectful and never chose his words carefully. If it were up to him, he would have put a full clip inside the young warrior's face. He didn't understand why they insisted on ceasing the war for three months. He wondered why it was so significant. Even so, he wanted Jimmy, bad.

"Kammron, why don't you grab your Moët, and bring it inside? We need to form some sort of understanding before we move forward in any way. There are still a lot of questions that need to be answered."

Kammron watched one of the Cuban chicks from earlier bend the other one over and stick her face in the other girl's pussy. She held her ass cheeks wide open while her face went from side to side. The other female was moaning loudly and telling her to keep going in Spanish.

"Yo', it seems like out here is where it's cracking at. Fuck we finna go all the way in the mansion for? I'd rather watch these hoes fuck each other than sit back and look at y'all ugly ass faces. Them thotties look like they getting it in. I say we stay out here and enjoy the view." Kammron looked into the pool again and shook his head.

The other Cuban was moaning so loud by this point that he wanted to walk over just to have an up-close and personal view. He started to walk in that direction when Showbiz stepped in his way. Kammron looked into his eyes with anger.

Showbiz was nearly forehead to forehead with him. "Say, Dunn, I understand you're used to doing things your way, but right now, you're on Vega turf, and this is how we conduct bidness down here in Havana. If you wanna do bidness wit' us, you gon' have to abide by the rules, that's just that." Showbiz clenched his teeth. He had visions of taking Kammron out of the game. For some reason, he just didn't like Harlem niggas. He wondered if it stemmed from his utter disdain for Jimmy.

Kammron placed his forehead against his. "Nigga, I don't follow nobody's rules, and you ain't gon' keep looking at me like you crazy either. It's something about you I don't like, and if you wanna do bidness wit' me you gon' have to change that shit."

Showbiz mugged him harder. "Nigga, fuck you, if it was up to me, I'd blow Harlem off the map with no hesitation."

Kammron pushed him as hard as he could out of his face, and upped two .40 Glocks. "Fuck you saying, Rich Boy?"

Duke jumped up from the table with his hand under his shirt clutching the handle of his Desert Eagle. He saw the Vega's bodyguards rushing toward Kammron and was confused as to what to do. He didn't know if he should shoot at them or wait. One thing was for sure his trigger finger was itching. The bodyguards surrounded Kammron with their guns out. They aimed at his head ready to put him down.

Kammron saw them and laughed. "You muthafuckas pull those triggers and I'ma light Showbiz's ass up like a Christmas tree."

Duke pulled both Desert Eagles out now and climbed on top of the umbrella table. The beams on the top of his firearms went from each security personnel. "Back the fuck up off the Kid and let us make our way up out of this joint."

Kammron cocked his hammers. "That's alright, Duke. These mafuckas pull them triggers and there's no longer going to be a fight over the Vega throne. I'ma crown a successor, right here, right now." He lowered his eyes into slits and felt the beats of his heart speed up.

Tristan bumped Showbiz out of the way and held up his right hand. "Calm down, Kammron, we're all friends here.

Ain't no need for none of this nonsense. We're here to get an understanding."

Showbiz shook his head in scorching anger. "Fuck that! Ain't no understanding coming from this fuck nigga, right here. We don't need to roll wit' these Harlem niggas at all. We're Vegas, we'll roll over them. Get these sorry muthafuckas off this island within the next thirty minutes, or I swear to God, I'll have them slain, and filleted into bitch nigga strips." Showbiz was so angry he was sweating along the side of his face.

"But Showbiz, what about, Jimmy and his Jamaican crew? Kammron is the only man we can get that close to penetrating him without an all-out war jumping off."

Showbiz dismissed his words with a wave of his hands. "I said what I said. Fuck Harlem, get rid of them!" His guards rushed both Kammron and Duke.

Kammron aimed at them. "Yo', y'all keep ya filthy hands to ya self. Any mafucka touch me I'ma splash him. Word to Uptown." Kammron snatched the duffle bag containing seven hundred thousand dollars off the ground before they were led out of the Vega palace inside of a crowd of security men.

Tristan stepped up to Showbiz and leaned into his ear. "You just cost us our only stronghold of Harlem. I hope you're happy with yourself." He brushed past Showbiz and disappeared inside the house.

Showbiz didn't give a fuck. The way he saw it, war was the only solution, and he was cool with that.

Chapter 6

Instead of connecting with the Vegas', Kammron utilized one of Duke's plugs from Brooklyn. His name was Kaleb, Kaleb was born and raised in The Redhook Houses. He had an arm that reached all the way to Vietnam, back to Chicago, and across to New York. He was a steady plug that gave them bricks of China for fifteen apiece. The China was without steps, and from the original fifteen thousand that was invested Kammron was able to make sixty gees off each brick.

For Harlem that was a turnover that was worth getting excited about, so he went into action. He snatched up all the starving project kids that he was familiar with and put them on. He gave them a pack and told them what he expected back from each one, and what their consequences would be if they fucked the packs off. He even put on a bunch of single mothers that were looking to make ends meet for their struggling family if a person was willing to get down to the nitty-gritty with Kammron he was ready to give them a shot. He figured the more work he put out there the more money he could make for the long run.

Jimmy was too busy focusing all his time and energy on Queens. Kammron didn't give a fuck about Queens, all he cared about was getting rich, and putting Harlem back on the map, so he went hard as he possibly could. Day in, and day out, he spent grinding with the ghetto low lives and cutthroats to make them coins add up. In two months, he was rocking, and rolling, and caught a plug with a Columbian named Ponchie who gave him bricks of coke for eight apiece. Ponchie and Duke's mother were fuckin' around on the low, and Ponchie had taken a particular liking to Kammron because of his hustle.

Ponchie got bricks directly from his father back in Columbia. Ponchie's father had twenty acres of a coke field that he'd inherited after his father passed away. The plug was gorgeous and extremely beneficial for Kammron. So much so, he opened trap houses all over Harlem, and Staten Island. He even had dread heads, and Goth kids pushing pure white for him on their college campuses.

Duke was more than street smart, he was also book smart. He was able to take the profits Kammron was seeing and helped him invest in the businesses all around Harlem. Kammron would give each business a distinct amount of money for them to add to their weekly intake of profits, and then he would give them a certain percentage of the money that they'd washed over for him. Businesses like laundromats and vending machines, restaurants, car washes, and even supermarkets were all places he targeted in order to wash his money clean.

Duke told him no matter what he did, he always had to make sure Uncle Sam always got his cut from the profits. The government was more susceptible to raiding and bringing down an empire if the person sitting at the head of the throne didn't pay his or her proper share in taxes. It was just the way the game went. As long as you were hitting those in power you had a better chance of staying around for a long time.

Kammron took heed to this and really went hard. There wasn't a business in Harlem he didn't penetrate. If he fell into resistance, he made that business pay with underhanded schemes. He had the local youth harass and vandalize businesses that refused to cooperate. He had the owners beaten senseless, and when push really came to shove he resorted to arson. His heart remained cold. He was finally starting to feel like the King of Harlem. His plugs were steady flowing, and the money was constant.

Kamina set him up with offshore accounts all over the globe. Helped him to understand the Stock Market and hired him two stockbrokers that were lethal insiders. Slowly but surely Kammron began to amass a strong amount of fortune. The money came so fast he didn't know what to do with it. He felt untouchable, powerful, like God. Duke did as much as he could to keep Kammron honest, and humble, but it was no easy task. Kammron was cocky, arrogant, and extremely flashy by every sense of the word. He was Harlem bred, and Harlem fed. Flamboyance was part of the culture in Uptown, and Kammron had adopted the disease like no other.

When Yasmin was in her fourth month of pregnancy, Kammron pulled up to the Obstetrician's office rolling a cherry and black Lamborghini that had his face in the paint, with Gucci peanut butter leather seats, and it was sitting on thirty-inch gold rims. He flipped open the doors and stepped out in fitted in Gucci, with a million dollars' worth of jewelry around his neck. The sun seemed to set on his jewels and glistened off them.

Yasmin was on her way to her car when Kammron blocked her path. He had a van full of hittas that followed him around at all times now. They were Harlem heavy hitters, cold-blooded killers, that would never hesitate to pop them cannons. Kammron made sure he'd handpicked them. When Yasmin saw Kammron her eyes got big as saucers. She looked him up and down before her eyes roamed all over the Lamborghini. Then she sucked her teeth and waved him off. She tightened her hold on Yazzy's hand and proceeded to load her into the car.

Kammron waited until Yazzy was in the car, and Yasmin had closed the door before he took a hold of her hand and turned her facing him. "What's good, Shorty?"

Yasmin sighed and crossed her arms. Light snow began to fall from the sky. There was a harsh wind that blew from east to west bringing on a chill that made both of them uncomfortable. "What's up, Kammron? I haven't heard from you in a few weeks. I thought you was finally over messing with me?" She didn't know why she said what she had. It wasn't like she missed him or anything, at least that's what she wanted to convince herself.

Kammron shook his head, and took hold of her arms, holding her. "N'all Goddess, it ain't nothin' like that. I been out here making shit happen. Somebody gotta do it. Jimmy missing in action, Bonkers still down for the count. Harlem is on my shoulders, I gotta stand up and make it twerk. I gotta bunch of shit situated now, and I'm ready to hold shit down. So, what's really good?"

Yasmin frowned and placed her hand on her stomach. "I mean first off you just missed the appointment, but since you didn't ask, I'm doing quite well. The baby is strong and healthy. I'm taking my vitamins, and other than him making me sick all the time, I feel like this pregnancy is going to be a breeze." She opened her car door with the intentions on getting inside it, leaving Kammron standing there looking stupid in the parking lot.

Kammron grabbed her left arm. "Look, Goddess, a mafucka sorry. I shoulda been here for you and I wasn't. Let me make it up to you?"

Yasmin looked into his eyes. "Yeah, and how are you going to do that?" Even though she felt she didn't care, she was curious to know what he had up his sleeve.

Kammron shrugged his shoulders. "Look, I don't know. You want me to buy you a new whip a something? Jewelry— a house? You wanna shut down the mall? I don't give a fuck what I gotta do as long as in the end, you'll forgive me."

Yasmin felt emotional and didn't know why. She couldn't believe Kammron was willing to submit to her in the fashion he was. As much as she didn't want to care about him, Bonkers had been laid up in the hospital for so long she felt confused. She craved manly attention, and she didn't even care if it was from Kammron.

"Yo', I'm good, Kamm. I appreciate the offer though, but I gotta get back home so I can go over these numbers for the business. You know how that goes. It was nice seeing you, though."

Kammron tightened his grip on her arm and leaned into her face. "Yo', Yasmin, stop tryna shit on a nigga? I'm trying as hard as I can, right now. I'm really trying to fuck wit' you, but all you're doing is getting me vexed." He sniffed her neck and laid kisses along the side of it, before biting into it.

Yasmin cringed, and let out a soft moan. Her middle became instantly moist. She hated it for doing so. She had remained conscious of Yazzy in the car. She pushed Kammron off her a short way, but he closed the distance quickly and held her close.

"Stop boy, don't you see my daughter in the car?" She questioned, feeling his hand run up and down the crotch of her jeans.

Kammron placed his lips on her ear. "I don't give a fuck about none of that. I want you, Yasmin, you already know how I am. If I want, you right the fuck now, I'll take that shit and make you deal wit' it. Ain't nobody got that snapper like you, and I'm feeling for you." He cuffed her pussy through her jeans and sucked on her neck.

Yasmin closed her eyes and inadvertently opened her legs further to feel him better. Her moaning increased. Her tongue traced the expanse of her lips. Then Yazzy knocked on the window of the car snapping her out of her zone. She jumped and turned around. Her ass was right in Kammron's lap.

"What's the matter, Baby?" She could feel him throbbing, it both excited, and irritated her.

Yazzy wrapped her arms around her body. "I'm cold, Mama? Can you turn on the heat if you're going to be out there for a minute?" She asked, shaking.

Yasmin backed all the way up against Kammron to push him backward, then she opened the door, and stuck the key in the ignition, turning on the engine. She felt Kammron take a hold of her hips, then he was grinding into her backside. "There you go, Baby. I'll be just a few more minutes." She pushed back into him and stood up.

Kammron took a step back. "Yo', Yasmin, come out and fuck wit' me tonight. Seriously, I just wanna spend a lil' time with you. You can at least grant me that?"

She smiled and shook her head. "I wish I could, Kammron, but I just got so much work to catch up on with the business. The investors are on me every second about every little thing. I gotta stay on top of stuff or when Bonkers wakes up we won't have a business."

Kammron released her. "Man fuck them businesses. Y'all got three salons, and y'all ain't making in a year what I'm making in one trap house in a month. Fuck them salons, you ain't gotta work no more. You got my kid inside of you now you're straight."

Yasmin opened the door and sat inside the car. "I wish I could, Kammron, but I gotta keep the businesses afloat. That's all we got, right now. I mean I appreciate what you're saying, but at the same time, I know my responsibilities. I have to stand on my own two feet as a woman. First, I'm finna go see Bonkers, then I gotta jump on the business. I got your number,

as soon as I'm done taking care of things, I'll send you a text."
She sat in the car and closed the door.

Kammron watched her back out of the parking spot and pulled away. He was so heated he felt like bussing at her whip. He pulled his nose and sniffed at the air.

Duke jumped out of the van that had been following Kammron on security. He walked up to Kammron and placed his hand on his shoulder. "Yo', you a'ight, bruh?"

Kammron shook his head. "Hell n'all, I want all three of that bitch's businesses burnt to the ground tonight. then their house. Matter fact do the house first while she at the hospital, then the salons. I'm tired of playing games, make this shit happen, Duke."

Duke nodded and patted him on the shoulder. He jogged back to the van and gave his troops the order to mount up. Kammron continued to watch Yasmin's whip until she disappeared from the parking lot. He felt irritated and vengeful.

T.J. Edwards

Chapter 7

Later that night, Kammron pulled up to the scene of the fire three cars deep. He jumped out of his Benz a half of block away from Yasmin's house and saw her breakout running to him. He wanted to laugh so hard, but maintained the mug on his face, as he opened his arms to receive her. She crashed into him and hugged him tightly with tears streaming down her face.

"Kammron, Kammron, oh my, God? They burned down our house and the three salons. I don't know what to do," she sobbed.

Kammron's mug intensified. "Who the fuck did this? Who burned them down?" he asked even though he already knew.

Yasmin shook her head from side to side. "I don't know who would do such a thing. I'm so tired. Why won't Bonkers just wake up? I feel so lost, right now."

He held her up, and wrapped his arms securely around her frame? Her baby bump poked into him, and it felt comforting. "Yasmin where is, Yazzy, is she okay?"

She nodded. "Yeah, she's with my mother. I got a text while I was at the hospital that these things had taken place, but you know how the reception is there. I didn't find out what was good until I left the building, then all four texts popped up at one time. Kammron, who would attack us like this? It's not fair, it's just not fair. I feel so sick, I don't know what to do. I wish Bonkers was awake."

Kammron felt that was a shot to him as a man. He hated the way every time something happened she spoke about Bonkers being the hero. He wanted her to see him in that light. His ego was getting the better of him, he hugged her tighter. "Don't worry about nothin', I got you, Goddess. After you finish hollerin' at all of these people, I'ma take you home and give you a bath, allow you to lean back. Is that okay, can I cater to you? Can we figure all of this shit out another day?"

Yasmin was crying hard, she shook her head. "I'm so lost— I'm so so lost!"

****

Three hours later, Kammron lit the last candle and set it along the rim of the tub. Then he stood up and guided Yasmin from the living room to the bathroom. He led her inside and stripped her. Once she was fully naked, he kneeled before her and kissed her stomach all over, then laid his face on it.

"You're having our baby, Yasmin. That's a lil' me and you in there, I can't wait." He planted more kisses all over her.

Yasmin wiped away her tears and rested her hands on the top of his head. "Aahh Kammron, boy what is wrong with you?" She didn't understand where his admiration was coming from, but she appreciated him being there to hold her down because nobody else could.

She had no idea how she was going to make ends meet, or how she was going to restore their businesses. She was being told the salons were completely ruined, one of them had actually exploded, and caused two other businesses on the block to catch fire. She was so worried that the perpetrators would seek out to kill her and Yazzy. This terrified her. She didn't know why she'd been targeted, but she only prayed the worst was behind her.

"Why are you here for me, right now, Kammron? Where is, Shana?"

Kammron kissed up her stomach and stood before her. He peered into her pretty brown eyes and moved her hair out of the way. "I ain't thinking about Shana, right now. Shana is good, the only person on my mind, right now is you. Just let me be here for you, Yasmin. Is that so hard?" He rubbed the side of her face and kissed her lips.

Yasmin closed her eyes and allowed him to try his best to heal her. Bonkers continuously crossed her mind, but now instead of their being visions of him with his arms wrapped around her, or them somewhere doing things romantically, she envisioned him in a hospital bed with a tube down his throat. The imagery was enough to break her down, then she became angry.

Kammron dropped to his knees again and spaced her thighs apart. He sniffed her pudgy sex lips and kissed them. Then swiped his tongue up and down her groove. "I'm here for you, right now, Yasmin. Everything is about you, I just wanna make you happy." He smushed her pussy lips together and sucked them into his mouth, slurping loudly.

"Unnhhh!" Yasmin moaned and placed her foot on the rim of the tub. It bumped a candle and caused it to fall into the water and go out.

She gripped Kammron's head with both hands and humped into his face. She needed to let go. She didn't want to think about her current reality. It was too much for one woman to contemplate figuring out on her own. Maybe Kammron was supposed to have her back. Maybe it was meant for them to become friends at the very least. She moaned again.

Kammron felt her peach's juices leaking down his chin. He didn't know why he loved the taste of Yasmin so much, but whenever he looked at her the first thing that came to his mind was tasting her pussy. It was crazy, and something he couldn't explain. He slipped two fingers into her and ran them in and out of her slowly. "I love this pussy, Yasmin. I love this pussy so so much."

She shivered and jerked into his mouth. She felt weak, as the ripples coursed through her and tears spilled down her cheeks. "You said you was going to cater to me, Kammron. You said you were going to put me into the tub and wash me up. What happened to all of that?" She moaned and humped forward into his mouth again. His administering felt so good to her.

Kammron sucked on her clitoris. His tongue flicked at her bud over and over. She shivered again and released a flood of juices onto his lips. Kammron sipped from her valley and swallowed her secretions. He pulled his fingers out and sucked them into his mouth. They tasted like her.

"Yo', you're right, Ma, that's what I told you. I'ma stand on that." He picked her up while she continued to shake slightly and placed her into the tub. He added just a bit of hot water and dipped his towel into the water. Then ran it across her shoulders and her neck.

Yasmin laid her head back and closed her eyes. "Why do you care so much, Kammron? All of a sudden you're doing things you've never done before. What is all of this about?" She asked feeling emotionally unstable.

Kammron kissed her forehead and rubbed the side of her face. "On some real shit, Yasmin, I've always been crazy about you. I just ain't know how to express that shit. I mean we was all young anyway, then when bro started someone on one shit wit' you, I ain't know how to handle that, but I rolled with the punches. Now I just wanna be a part of you, I mean more than my shorty growing inside of you, too." He kissed her forehead again and started to wash her body from her pretty toes, to the base of her neck. The entire time he maintained a hard-on, fiending for her womb.

Yasmin looked him over through the glares of the candle. The flickering fire made his shadows dance on the walls. He smelled of Gucci cologne. She hated herself once again for feeling so safe around him. She knew Kammron was a beast.

She also knew, he had a baby mama at home, and they barely got along. She felt nothing positive could ever come from the two of them fuckin' around, but at the moment she just wanted to be free, and unattached to Bonkers. Unattached to the businesses that had gone up in flames. She wanted it to be about her, and that's what he was making it.

"Kammron, I honestly don't know what's going on, but I just want you to know, I appreciate you for being here, and for inviting me into your home tonight. I'm going through a lot, and I could really use a shoulder. You really stepped up to the plate for me. I can never thank you enough for comforting me, I sincerely mean that."

Kammron shrugged his shoulders and began rubbing her stomach. "I got you, Yasmin, from here on out I got you. I don't give a fuck what goes on, I'ma hold you down like a Don is supposed to. All I ask is that you give me a chance. I mean what do you have to lose?"

She smiled. "Other than Bonkers coming too and killing both of our asses? I don't know, I don't want to cross him in more ways than I already have. I mean, I'm supposed to be more of a woman than that."

Kammron tried to calm himself from getting irritated. It seemed like every time she mentioned something about Bonkers he found himself heated. He loved his homie, but Yasmin was doing something to him. He felt like he wanted her to himself. "Yo', check this out, Yasmin. I ain't tryna replace, Bonkers. That's yo' nigga, I can respect that. But as long as he is out of commission you belong to me. I mean that shit, you're my bitch, and I'll kill a nigga over yo' ass. Word is bond. You carrying my seed, and it's on me to make sure you have the best of the best. If I gotta cash you out then so be it. Fuck them salons! Word to, Kathy man, I'ma cop you a few new spots and let you be the Queen of them bitches. I wanna see you get ya shine on like, Killa Kamm, it's only right. You hear what the fuck I'm saying to you?"

Yasmin smiled and nodded. That thuggish side of Kammron did something to her middle. Now he was acting all possessive, and it was driving her nuts. She felt so ashamed. She was Bonkers' woman, she belonged to him, not Kammron. So, she wondered why him being possessive over her drove her so crazy?

"Yeah, I hear you! But is that really, right?"

Kammron shrugged his shoulders. "I don't know, and I don't give a fuck. I'm feeling you, and the God gotta have you. It's as simple as that." He slid his hand between her thighs and rubbed her pussy. The lips felt slippery as his middle finger slipped in between her folds. Her hot hole wrapped around it and seemed to roast him. "Damn, yo pussy hot, Yasmin."

She raised her knee. "Shut up, I already know that. Why you got yo finger in there anyways?"

Kammron was stroking his piece. "I'ma be honest with you, I need some of this box. I'm sitting here trying to be as humble as I possibly can. We can make it all about you, but baby I need some of this pussy, right now. It's calling, Daddy." He grabbed her under the arms, lifted her up and pulled her out of the tub. Then made her wrap her thighs around him. "Reach under there, and put me inside of you, hurry up."

Yasmin hesitantly reached behind her and felt his hot penis throbbing inside of her little hand. She squeezed it and inserted it into her box. Her eyes rolled into the back of her head, as she slid down on to him. It didn't take long for him to fill her up. He bounced her up a down slowly and methodically. Plunging into the deepest regions of her center.

Kammron kept his eyes trained on her face as he fucked Yasmin, with each stroke he grew more and more attached.

He relished in the way her face contorted with pleasure and pain. It felt so good he began to make noises of his own. "Yasmin, just me, unnhh-unnhhh! Just me dis my pussy—mine—just mine!" He continued to bounce her up and down.

Yasmin threw her head all the way back and moaned with reckless abandonment. All pretenses of her not enjoying the act were thrown to the wind. It was good, she couldn't deny it. She allowed Kammron to dick her down for an entire hour. Then he washed her body from head to toe once again and fucked her hard from the back in the shower, before carrying her naked to his master bedroom where he rubbed her down with lotion, and oils, before curling up with her possessively, and falling asleep. The last words Yasmin heard before she drifted off was him telling her she belonged to him, and only him. Then he kissed her all over her face.

T.J. Edwards

Chapter 8

If Kammron never respected Duke before, Duke forced him to respect his hustle in the weeks that followed. In a matter of weeks that followed the arson, Duke flooded Harlem with trap houses and China white Bandos. It got to the point that every section of the borough had at least one or more buildings that belonged to Kammron, buildings that popped both narcotics. They had long soup lines stemming from each establishment that Kammron's workers were forced to keep orderly. The Coke spots were jumping like Zion Williams. Kammron would have half of the apartments push pure white, and the other half pumped hard rock. The plug from Columbia was steady, and the work remained pure. So pure it tingled the finger at each touch. Kammron put Duke in charge of everything white, and rocky.

Duke took his position to heart. He made it his bidness to grow the operations he was put ahead of. So much so that Kammron was forced to allow Duke to oversee the China side of things as well. Kammron trusted him and knew he could depend on Duke to continue handling bidness. Not only was Duke a chemist in the kitchen, but when it came to that beef shit, he was quick to clap at a nigga as if they were at a recital. Duke was good at keeping the beef low, and the money intake high.

He always told Kammron it was impossible for anybody to make money, and beef at the same time. So, he did all he could to keep the beef shit with any outsiders to a minimal. It was all about them attaining mass riches. Duke had a daughter to feedback in Philly, and when it came down to his daughter there was nothing he wouldn't do for her safety and well-being. His goal was to make sure she never wanted for anything. Her name was Nila, and she was the love of his life.

But weeks turned into months, and late into the winter Duke came to Kammron with his first bit of drama concerning a group that seemed to be plotting to come up against Kammron's regime. He summoned Kammron two blocks over from Ruckers, and down into the basement of one of the apartment buildings where there were a male and a female seated at the table smoking a cigarette. Kammron stepped past fifteen of his security men before he was able to enter into the downstairs portion of the building. The basement was swampy and smelled of piss, cigarette smoke, and alcohol.

Kammron walked right up to the long table and slammed his tool kit down on it. He opened the kit and glanced over to Duke. "Fuck do we have here, Duke?"

Duke came and stood beside him. "One of the traps got shot up and ran in last week. We lost two birds, and word is there is a new crew in town from Yonkers that's thinking it's sweet. The Hittas picked up this pussy nigga, right here, and this bitch. They supposed to be a part of that crew and refuse to answer questions on where the yayo is, and who took it. Since that's the case I think it's only fair we show em how we get down in Black Mecca." Duke smiled and mugged the pair.

The female grunted, she was dark-skinned, with brown eyes. Her hair was pulled back into a ponytail. She rocked a Nike jumpsuit overall black low top Air Force Ones. "Say, Kid, fuck y'all think y'all about to do to us down here?"

Kammron slapped on his black latex gloves and laughed. "Bitch, you finna find out now ain't you?"

The female's light-skinned buddy looked nervous. "Say, B, we just moved over here. Ain't nobody even fuckin' wit' you Uptown niggas like that. Word is bond, all of this shit ain't nothing but a huge misunderstanding."

Kammron curled his upper lip. "Who slugged up my trap, and where are my bricks?"

The female mugged him. "I don't know how you niggas get down out here in Harlem, but in Yonkers, if a bitch opens her mouth she gets her lips cut off. I ain't trying to have that happen, so do what the fuck you gon' do and get this shit over with. Word up."

Kammron laughed and smiled at her. She had balls, he liked that. In addition to her heart, she was also really pretty in that project Goddess kind of way. "That's the way you feel, Goddess?"

"That's exactly the way I feel, and I'm sure my brother do, too," she retorted looking her sibling over. "Right, Ken?"

Her brother Ken looked nervous. He wiped sweat from his forehead and swallowed. "Yo', what the fuck you doing with a jar of peanut butter, Kid?"

Kammron snapped his fingers, and Duke and three of the Harlem hittas snatched up Ken and slammed him to the wall. Kammron smiled, and dug his fingers into the peanut butter, and scooped up a nice portion of it. He walked over to Ken and stood in from of him. "Open yo' mafuckin' mouth."

Ken clamped down on his teeth. He shook his head from side to side, groaning deep within his throat. He struggled against Kammron's henchmen.

Kammron waited impatiently. "I said open yo' mafuckin' mouth, now nigga!" His hittas upped their firearms and aimed them at Ken's face. The young man opened his mouth right away, and Kammron dumped the huge glob of peanut butter into his gullet.

Ken chewed it at first, he got it full of spit, then he swallowed. The huge amount got stuck in his throat. He watered his mouth as much as possible and swallowed as hard as he could. The peanut butter slowly oozed down and felt like it was choking him.

Kammron sat across the table from the female. "This how this shit finna go. You gon' tell me who shot up my trap, and where my bricks are, or you're going to watch your brother be suffocated by this government peanut butter." The peanut butter came from an all-white can that had two big peanut shells on it. Its hue was dark brown, and it smelled bad.

The dark-skinned female looked across the basement at her brother. It looked like Ken was struggling to breathe. She became worried. "Yo', this shit ain't got nothin' to do with us, B. Why you, niggas can't take this up with God nem?"

Kammron looked her over for a moment. "Is that your final answer?"

She mugged him and looked off. "That rat shit ain't in me, Kid. Give me what I got coming and bury me. Fuck y'all, word to my mother in heaven."

Kammron scooted away from the table after scooping up a ridiculous amount of peanut butter. He walked up to Ken and grabbed him by the mouth. "Open this ma'fucka, Dunn, since yo' sister don't wanna say nothing you gon' suffer the consequences. He forced Ken's teeth apart and smeared the peanut butter all on his tongue, and Duke came and slapped a piece of duct tape over his mouth, and nose.

Ken began to chew, and panic, he couldn't breathe. He struggled against the Hittas and hollered. Tears ran down his cheeks. He felt the peanut butter ooze down, and lodge itself into the middle of his throat. Once there it slid southern until it bumped against the other peanut butter that was already there. He took a deep breath, and a portion of it went down the wrong pipe. He began to choke, and his heart skipped beats. His lungs contracted, then he was hysterical. Duke held him with a mug on his face, Ken's head was turning blue.

Kammron came and sat across the table from Ken's sister. "You got something you wanna tell me?"

She eyed her brother with serious concern. She didn't want to be responsible for his death, but at the same time they couldn't go out like ducks. Yonkers had raised her better than that. She was from Tarantino, the heart of Yonkers. The slum of the slums. If she opened, her mouth she risked her entire family meeting their demise.

"Why don't you let my brother go and you can do whatever the fuck you wanna do to me?" she suggested.

Ken felt his chest on fire. He took a deep breath, and his right lung exploded. It felt like a sharp pain in his chest. His eyes flooded with water, and his nose bled. He became limp against the men that were holding him. He could taste blood on his tongue, it coupled with the peanut butter. His eyes got as big as saucers while he shook as if he was having a seizure.

Kammron tapped the table and stood up. He stepped in front of Ken and watched him choke nearly to death. "Say, Goddess, it looks like yo' brother on his way out. You better open up them big pretty lips and say something."

Her eyes misted over. "It's all part of the game. We both knew what we were getting into when we entered into this life. Ashes to ashes, dust to dust. Kill him first and bury me next. Word to the heavens." She stared off into the distance, feeling somewhat remorseful.

Kammron eyed her with extreme admiration. He had to take a trip through Yonkers. If they made females as hard as the one before him, he knew it would be in his best interest to plug with a few killas from out that way.

"A'ight then, y'all sit back and watch his bitch ass kill over then." Kammron grabbed him by the throat and ripped the duct tape away and blood seeped from his lips.

He cleaned the rest of the can of peanut butter clumping it into Ken's mouth. Then he taped him back and stood at a safe distance while Ken went crazy.

Ken's final lung collapsed, it sounded like a balloon had been popped. His chest caved in, and his heart pounded five times real hard before it lethally spasmed and stopped. He groaned as loud as he could, then everything faded to black. Duke and their Hittas released him and allowed him to fall forward.

His sister beat her hand on the table and wiped her tears from her face. "Dat all you pussy niggas got?"

Kammron stood in front of her and lowered his eyes. "You still gon' maintain yo silence, huh?"

She looked up at Kammron and snickered. "You muthafuckin' right." She hawked a loogie and it blew off right into his left eye. The yellow substance stung him with its heat. It slid down his face and dripped off of his chin.

Kammron was disgusted. He wiped away the spit and broke into a fit of laughter. "You got heart, right? Yo,' shit beat that Savage shit, right?"

She was ready to die, ready for whatever they were going to do to her. She simply wanted to get it over with. "Do whatever you gonna do? I don't fear you or no man. Only Jehovah can judge me."

Kammron laughed. "Ain't that the truth?" He could still feel the spot on his cheek where she had spit on him. He grabbed a pair of pliers from his toolbox and snapped his finger.

The Hittas rushed over, and picked her up, just like Ken they held her against the wall. "Let me go you muthafuckas! Get ya filthy hands off me." She struggled against them and tried her best to fight them away with no success.

Kammron stepped in front of her and slapped some duct tape across her lips. "I see you one of them nasty lil' project hoes? Spitting and doing all that type of shit. It's all good though before it's all said and done you finna tell me what's really good with my trap. You gon' see." He took the pliers, clamped them on to the tip of her nose, squeezed them as hard as he could and pulled backward, taking a large portion of her nose with him? The skin slid off and exposed her bloody bone. She had never been in so much pain. She closed her eyes and jumped into the air even though there were three dudes holding her. She screamed as loud as she could into the duct tape and prayed for death.

Kammron stood right in front of her waving the skin flap in her face. "You ready to tell me what's really good?"

She continued to scream into the tape. When she opened her eyes and saw her dark brown skin inside the pliers it was like the pain intensified even more. She blacked out for a split second and came back to.

Kammron pulled the tape back and rubbed the side of her face. "Who ran in my trap shorty? Ain't no sense in being a hero."

She huffed and puffed. "Go fuck yourself Harlem. Kill me like you just did my brother. I ain't got nothing else to say to you." She closed her eyes and awaited the inevitable.

Kammron's mind was completely blown. He could not believe a female could have as much heart as she was displaying. As much as he wanted to finish her off it was like something in him just couldn't do it. He took a step back, turned to Duke, grabbed his arm and led him into the far corner of the basement. "Yo', check this out, I'm finna let shorty go."

Duke jerked back his head. "You finna do what, Kid? Are you crazy? She missing a whole ass piece of nose."

Kammron smiled and shook his head. "Calm down, Dunn, I ain't saying it like that. I'm saying I'm finna let her go, right now, but I want you to follow her. It don't matter what we do to her she ain't finna say shit. She stomped down, bruh. The only way we gon' find out who it is behind all of this is if she leads us directly to them. So once again, I'm finna let her go, use that, Kamina." He rested his hand on Duke's shoulder.

Kamina was Kammron's attorney and business partner of sorts. He had plugs on all types of devices because Kamina's wife was actually a Federal agent. When he referred to hitting her with the Kamina he spoke regards to a tracking device.

Duke pulled at the hairs of his chin and nodded. He saw where Kammron was coming from and did his best to make some sense of it. "A'ight, I got you, Killa, do yo thing."

Kammron walked back into the area of the basement where she was. He looked her over one last time. Blood dripped from her face. She breathed loudly the blood was clogging the airwaves in her nostrils. More than once she blew of out, and it landed on the top of her silver tape.

"Yo', shorty, you free to go. I can honor an Earth that keeps her mouth shut. He tossed a handkerchief at her. "Clean yo self and get the fuck out of here."

Her eyes opened widely. She felt confused as if she knew he had something up his sleeve. She hollered into the tape to get his attention. Duke ripped the tape from her lips, shook the blood from his leather glove and stood back. She spits on the basement floor and wiped her mouth.

"I ain't going nowhere unless you let me take my brother's body with me as well. I'm not leaving him here with y'all so y'all can defile it. Let me give him a proper burial, he deserves it."

Duke looked up at Kammron and awaited his response. Kammron gave him the signal and turned his back on them. Duke snatched her up, and he, along with their troops removed her from the basement. She fought with them the whole way, when they made it into the backyard, Duke had plans of knocking her noodles on the pavement, but she took off running but not before he could place the tracking device that Kamina had given him on her belt.

Kammron packed away his tools, as a text came through on his phone from Jimmy. He was back in town, and he wanted to meet with him and Duke. Kammron laughed to himself. The last person he wanted to converse with was Jimmy. As far as he was concerned, they ain't have nothing to talk about. He texted him back and told him to name the time and place.

T.J. Edwards

Chapter 9

Kammron sat in his seat and fingered the good ropes on his neck. The crushed diamonds caused them to sparkle, and dance in the light. He was high as a kite and trying his best to keep from nodding out. He was fitted in Gucci from head to toe and rocked a fat ass gold Rolex on his left wrist dripping with yellow ice. It looked like he'd stuck his watch in a lemon snow cone. The Gucci shades were mirror tinted, just like the Porsche he'd pulled up to Jimmy's palace in. He pulled his nose and smiled at Duke, who in turn nodded his head at Kammron. He was fitted in all black with his hoodie pulled over his head. His shades were dark like Easy E's. He didn't like or trust Jimmy, so he was on high alert like the country whenever there is a terrorist attack.

Jimmy strolled into the big living room with two body-guards behind him. He carried a platter full of North Korean and set it on the table. There were three good straws on the platter as well.

When he sat down, he slid the platter across to Kammron. "Lil' homie, here you go, check that shit out."

The platter landed in front of Kammron, and he pushed it away. "That shit swag, I'm good. I got my own shit, and it's ninety-eight percent. I step on that shit the way I want too, not the other way around. Fuck you call this meeting for? Harlem ain't heard from you in an eternity."

Jimmy was offended. "Oh, so you live enough to push my shit away now?"

Kammron scoffed. "Nigga, I'm a muthafuckin' Boss now. Don't no nigga feed me crumbs, I eat top-notch, and until I'm full. Now once again, why the fuck you call this meeting?"

Duke watched Jimmy's mannerisms really closely. He knew Jimmy was about that life as well. He couldn't allow him to get the ups on him under no circumstances. He'd already sized up Jimmy's bodyguards. They were Jamaican and wore black paint on their faces.

Jimmy sighed and balled his fists. He took a deep breath and looked across the table at Kammron. "What's good with this free enterprising shit you got going on, Kammron? I thought we had a good thing, and you and Bonkers worked under me? I'm getting word back from some heavy hitters of the underworld that you're doing your own thing, and you actually had the audacity to go and meet with the Vegas without letting me know anything about it. Fuck type of shit is you on?"

Kammron adjusted his jewels, grabbed the Apple juice from the table, and took a sip. "First of all, nigga you can lower your muthafuckin' voice. I can hear yo yellow ass loud and clear. Secondly, nigga, I worked under you when I was a shorty in this game. I was naïve. Well, I ain't naïve no more. I'm a muthafuckin' vet, and I'm holding Harlem down like a Don is supposed to. I got the borough on my back, and I ain't going nowhere. Besides, you from Queens now. Uptown is for the Gods." Kammron pulled his nose and mugged Jimmy through his shades.

Jimmy was seething. "Nigga, don't get shit twisted. You see me coming at you all humble and shit, and you quick to take my kindness for weakness. That a be yo worst nightmare, Killa. The only reason I'm coming at you like I am is because we got history, and you are my brother's right hand. We're cool, always have been."

Kammron shook his head. "That's where you're wrong nigga, I ain't never been cool wit' you, Jimmy. I just used yo punk ass to get to where I needed to be. I ain't never liked you, or shit you stood for. Yousa selfish ass nigga always has been. The type of fuck nigga to live in a palace while his own brother scraped and scrounged in the slums. We wasn't eating we was nibbling nigga. But now—" Kammron held up his jewels and slammed his Porsche keys on the table. "The God eating and burping at the same time. They always said that I was gon' grow up to be nothing. Well, muthafucka thanks for nothing!" He laughed for a second and removed his glasses from his face. Now he was cold as ice. "Jimmy, Uptown belongs to me now. Nigga, I'm ready to die over my borough. I ain't finna let you, or no other nigga come and eat in my shit. Fuck you gotta say about that?"

Jimmy smiled and pulled the platter of raw over to him. He took two hard lines and threw his head back. Then he pinched his nostrils closed and held them. He felt the high take over him immediately. He still couldn't believe Kammron had become so big-headed, he actually had enough gall to sit in front of him and say the things he had. He knew that words weren't going to be enough to get his message across. He had other plans for Kammron. Every Capo kept an ace up his sleeve.

He decided to play it smooth. "I was born and bred in Harlem, Kammron. It beats in my soul just like it does yours."

"Nigga, you from Havana. You came over here later on? I was born in the slums right on a hunnit fortieth, and Lennox. Caught my first piece of pussy and popped my first nigga right on a hunnit forty fifth and Broadway. Then you came into the picture. So, don't try and be on the same level wit' me. I said what I said and that's just that. If you wanna do bidness in Harlem you hit me up, and we'll make arrangements. On the strength of, Bonkers, I ain't gon' get on no lethal shit wit' you, unless, you can't take heed to my warning about the severity of the situation. If you get on some hard-headed shit, it's on you."

"Mon fuck Dis boy, right now. Let me blast this, Bombaclat, and be on our way!" One of Jimmy's security men hollered reaching for the gun in his waistband.

Duke jumped up with two .40 Glocks and placed beams on both of Jimmy's guard's heads. He was seconds away from pulling his triggers. Kammron took another sip from his apple juice. "So, if we ain't got shit else to talk about, I'ma about to be on my way. I appreciate your time, Jimmy. I do hope you take heed to my advice and stay out of Harlem." He stood up and slid his shades back on his face. "We ready to die 'bout this, believe that." As he walked past Jimmy, he tapped him on the shoulder and broke into a fit of laughter. "Come on Duke, they don't want these problems."

****

Jimmy sat there for a full hour straight thinking things over after Kammron had left his home. He was vexed and had never been so mad in his life. Not only did he want revenge on Kammron, but he wanted him to suffer. He wanted to be the one at the hems making him beg for mercy. He hated the man with every fiber of his being, and low key always had. He nodded his head. "Yeah, I gotta trick for his ass. You better believe that" he said this out loud more so to himself than anyone else.

****

That night Kammron counted eight hundred thousand dollars by money machine while Yasmin sat across the living room from him and counted a full million in cash by the same use. He couldn't help looking across the room at her. She was only wearing a bra. Her stomach was all the way poked out and shining from the cocoa butter they'd rubbed on it. "I can't believe you got me over here counting all of this money, Kammron. I feel like a D boy or something." She laughed shaking her head.

Kammron blew a kiss at her. "I know this ain't you, but you rocking wit' me now until the homie pulls out of that coma. I gotta make sure you're straight. That's just how the game goes. This is Harlem finest over here, Yasmin. Now let me hear you call me, Daddy. You know I love to hear that shit coming from your mouth."

"Dad-dee." She laughed.

"Say it again," he ordered.

"Dad-dee-Dad-dee-Dad-dee," she repeated over and over.

Kammron dropped the ten-thousand-dollar pile of cash from his hand and crawled across the floor toward her like a Lion. When he made it to her, he kissed up her stomach and rubbed his face all over it. "Shorty you driving me crazy, keep saying that shit."

She repeated it over and over again and opened her thighs. She knew what was coming next. He pulled her pink beater up her thighs and kissed up and down her sex lips. He opened them with his thumbs and sucked on her pearl. She jerked into his mouth and rolled her back. She held his head and moaned loudly. Kammron's tongue game was second to none as much as she hated to admit that.

He never failed to make her cum. "Kammron, what you tryna do, Daddy?"

Kammron was too busy running his tongue in and out of Yasmin's pussy. Her gap had become intoxicating to him, it was like he needed to taste her daily or his day didn't go right. He removed his face, and it was covered with her juices. He couldn't wait to hit her pregnant pussy. Kammron felt pregnant pussy was the best pussy in the world. He stroked himself, as he anticipated what Yasmin's insides were about to feel like.

Yasmin arched her back and opened her thighs as far as she could. Dug her nails into the arm of the couch and screamed as an orgasm rocked through her. Kammron continued to flick her clit with his tongue, sucking it, and nipping the bud with his teeth.

"Daddy! Daddy! Daddy! I'm cumming, Aaahhh shit, I'm cumming!" She began to squirt her juices into his mouth.

Kammron swallowed them and kept licking until he felt her shock waves dissipate. Then he grabbed a bundle of money from the table and threw it at her. "That's about a hunnit gees, it's yours. Huh, here go about a hunnit more. You my muthafuckin', baby mama. Bend that ass over and give, Daddy some of his baby pussy."

Yasmin got up and bent over the sofa. Her heavy belly protruded. She spread her legs, and looked back at him, waiting in anticipation. "Come on, Daddy, fuck yo, baby. Hit this pussy, right now!"

Kammron stroked his piece four more times and slid into her cave. Her heat enveloped him, her walls suffocated him and tugged as if they were hungry for his animal. He stroked in and out at full speed right away. Loving the feel of her skin slapping against his. Her scent drifted into his nostrils and drove him insane. He fucked her as hard as he could, watching the way her cheeks jiggled every time he slammed forward. The pregnancy had caused her to put on a few pounds that complimented her frame. She felt good, as he held her waist, and went to town.

Yasmin closed her eyes tightly and crashed back into him over and over, faster and faster. She could feel him plunging deeper and deeper and it felt amazing. She reached under herself and pinching and diddling her clit. That coupled with his deep strokes sent waves, and tremors through her.

"Unnhhh-nnhhh, Daddy, I'm finna—" She moaned and slammed as hard as she could into him.

The pregnancy had made her incredibly horny, and it didn't help matters that Kammron was always sucking on her or playing between her legs. She had never been more stimulated in all of her life. Kammron continued to long stroke, he dug deep, gripped her hips, and splashed back to back, groaning. Yasmin felt his hot jets, and came just as hard, falling to the sofa with him still jerking away on her back deep in her slot. After they finished their fuck session, Kammron, put all the money away in his safes and fell out next to Yasmin in the master bedroom.

****

That night, Kammron woke up to two masked men holding him down and slapping duct tape on his mouth. They held out his left arm, while another man placed his knee on his wrist to hold him steady. A masked Jimmy smiled and took the syringe from his inside coat pocket. It was filled with the best of the best North Korean. He found one of Kammron's thick veins and injected him, giving him half of it at one time.

Kammron felt the drug enter into his veins, and all of his senses went numb, before the sudden rush of euphoria took over him. Though he was ridiculously angry, he couldn't help smiling. The North Korean sent him on a journey like never before. Jimmy waited a moment, then hit him with another blast of the work. He pulled it out, and set the syringe on the lamp table, before ordering his men out of the room, and out of Kammron's house.

Yasmin waited until the men were out of the house for a full ten minutes before she snuck out of the closet and rushed to Kammron's side. "Baby, baby, wake up. What did they do to you?"

Kammron's eyes were crossed. He was in a far-away land of bliss. He smiled and ran his tongue across his lips. This was a whole new level of happiness. A level he never knew existed.

Chapter 10

"Ohhh—Ohhh!" Yasmin screamed holding her stomach and slowly walking down the hallway toward the bathroom. Her water had just broken and knew the baby was on its way. Her contractions were about two minutes apart. She needed to get to the hospital fast, or she was going to have the baby right on the living room floor.

"Kammron, Daddy, it's happening! Oh God, it's happening!"

Kammron flicked the syringe and rubbed his thick vein, before pricking the needle into it. He slid it in as deep as he had to, then pushed down on the feeder. As the poison entered his system his eyes rolled into the back of his head. He felt like he was having an orgasm.

He cheesed and groaned. "Fuck that's so good."

Yasmin crawled to the door and beat on the bottom of it. "Kammron, help me, Daddy. Help me, the baby is coming."

Kammron nodded out, his eyes closed, drool slid from the corner of his mouth and down his neck. He began to snore and scratch his arm as hard as he could. He smacked his lips, he could hear the sound of music playing loudly in his head. It was a soothing rhythm before he knew what was taking place, he'd nodded out.

Yasmin passed out, when she came to, she felt the baby making its way out of her. She sat up and screamed. "Kammron, help me, help me—hurry up!"

Duke opened the front door of the house at the hearing of Yasmin's screams. He pulled a 9mm out of his holster and rushed inside. He looked down the hallway and saw Yasmin sprawled on her back, with her thighs wide open. There was a puddle of water in the hall that he jumped over. When he got to her side, he kneeled beside her and took hold of her arm. "Sis, are you okay?"

She shook her head. "No, Duke, the baby is coming. He's here, I feel him coming out of me."

Duke cursed and slid around to the front of her. He looked down and saw Yasmin fully dilated. The baby's head was just beginning to crown. He cursed again. "Aaahhh shit, okay. Fuck, where that nigga, Kammron?"

Yasmin huffed and puffed, sweat creased her brow. He's in the bathroom passed out. I been beating on the door—he ain't answered," she said this through heavy breaths.

Duke braced himself, he rushed to the linen closet and pulled out a bunch of towels. He took one and placed it under her head, then one under her ass, and prepared to receive the baby. More of it had slid past her labials. Yasmin held her thighs wide open.

"Kammron, get yo ass out here, God. Yo', Yasmin having the baby!" Duke hollered. "Push sis, push as hard as you can."

Yasmin held her thighs and began to push. "Arrgh—arrgh—arrgh, fuck!"

Duke couldn't believe what he was witnessing. The baby slowly began to slide out. He saw its curly black hair. He placed his hands on the head to guide it out through the process. "Kammron, Killa, get yo ass out here, B! Word up, this shit is freaking me out!" Duke wanted to turn his head away but knew, he couldn't. "Push Yasmin, Kammron!"

Kammron's eyes popped open, he jerked and stood up. He wiped his nose, as the high continued to take over him. He coulda sworn somebody was calling him. He sat back on the toilet, with his eyes low. His vision was cloudy, his mouth felt dry as a desert. He grabbed his spoon and filled it with the China White, dropped water on top of it and lit the bottom of the spoon with a lighter until it started to bubble. Once it was good and bubbly, he stuck the tip of his needle inside of it and drew up the raw into his syringe. He sat it on the sink and tied the rope tighter around his arm until his vein popped up. He was just about to insert the needle when Duke hollered his name. Kammron dropped the syringe and pulled open the door of the bathroom. His eyes turned as big as paper plates when he saw the sight of Duke with his head between Yasmin's thighs.

"Yo,' fuck is you doing between my bitch's thighs?" Kammron grabbed the Glock from behind his back and cocked his hammer.

Duke mugged him. "Nigga, put that joint away. She having y'all baby, Kid. Get ya ass down here and help me deliver Shorty."

Kammron stood mugging him for a moment. His eyes trailed down to Yasmin's gap. When he saw the baby's head sticking halfway out, he dropped to his knees, and the pistol fell to the floor and went off.

Yasmin jumped, and her eyes bucked wide open. She growled and shook her head. "Uhhhh-uhhhh—arrgh!"

Kammron slid up her body and stayed by her side. He was so high that he could barely make out her face. He felt numb, even his lips were numb. "Baby, I'm here, Daddy right the fuck here. Just push for me, push for me so we can get this baby up out of you."

Yasmin pushed and pushed, she held her knees and screamed at the top of her lungs as sweat dripped from her chin. Her middle felt like she was being ripped in two. All she wanted was her son out of her. She wanted the labor to be over with.

****

Four hours later, Kammron staggered from the bathroom of the hospital after boosting his high. He stepped beside Yasmin and sat on the bed. Yasmin smiled and handed the baby to him wrapped in a black and red Gucci baby blanket. "Hold your son, baby. He looks just like you."

Kammron opened his eyes as wide as he could. He needed to shake the high off him. He looked down at the baby and could barely bring his eyes into focus. He looked him over and licked his lips. He saw so many of his features within the child. He even had his dimples.

"Yo', he looks just like me, I'm naming him Cokane call my lil' man's Coke for short."

Yasmin sat up and crossed her arms. "What, you think I'm finna let you name my baby after a fuckin' drug? Man, Kammron you done lost your mind."

Kammron bounced him up and down. "I don't give a fuck what you talking about. This is a male child, I'm in charge of naming him. His name is Cokane, and like I said we'll call him Coke for short."

Yasmin smacked her lips. "Kammron, I'm not letting you name him, Cokane. I'd rather it just be Coke then. I don't need him growing up with a first name like Cokane. At least meet me halfway. I mean your last name is already, King. Damn, give our son a chance."

Kammron stood up with the baby and bounced him up and down. "A'ight, I can do that, his name is Coke. Coke King. Hell yeah, I can see Harlem written all over that. Word to, Kathy in heaven." Kammron kissed the baby's forehead. "You hear that lil' homie? Your name is Coke King. You are the next legend of Harlem. First, it was your father, and now it's you." He hugged him to his chest and fell in love. Then walked over to Yasmin and kissed her cheek. "Thank you for this blessing, Goddess. Word to Jehovah, I appreciate you."

Yasmin was still upset by the child's name, but she played it off cool. "You're welcome, baby. All I ask is that you be an amazing father to your child. Give him more of a chance than you've ever had." She closed her eyes and yawned.

Shana stepped to the hospital room door and knocked three times, before turning the knob. She pushed it in with a fake smile on her face. She couldn't believe Yasmin's dirty ass had actually had the audacity to have a baby by her man. She wanted to spit in her face and knock her baby out of Kammron's hands. After all, he had not been home beside her in weeks. "Hey, there girl, I saw your mother's post about you on Facebook, and your mother told me where you were. She on her way up here, too. She's about fifteen minutes out."

"Shana, what the fuck is you doing up here? Don't start no bullshit," Kammron said dryly.

Shana didn't even look in his direction she was so disgusted with him. "Boy, ain't nobody come up here on no bullshit. I am perfectly fine, trust and believe that. Now anyway—" She walked over to Yasmin and took her hand. "How are you?"

Yasmin felt horrible, not only did she feel weak, and exhausted, but she was feeling super guilty for sleeping with Shana's man. She felt like a whore. She shrugged her shoulders. "I'm doing well! How about you?"

Shana scoffed and laughed to herself. "I'm fine. Do you mind if we talk a minute before your mother gets here?"

Yasmin sat up as far as she could. She adjusted her pillows and looked over at the heart monitoring machine. Her blood pressure was still a bit high, but it had lowered considerably. The same problem had occurred doing her birth with Yazzy. "Talking is fine, go ahead, I'm listening."

Shana cleared her throat and nodded her head over at Kammron. "I was wanting to know if we could talk alone?"

Kammron frowned. "Hell muthafuckin' n'all y'all can't. What the fuck you gotta say to her that you can't say in front of me? You gon' tell her that I whacked your sister again to see if she'll roll with you against me, huh, bitch?" Kammron was getting so angry he started holding the baby too tight. Coke began screaming at the top of his little lungs.

Yasmin reached for Coke and Kammron handed him over. She held her ripe nipple to his mouth, Coke latched on right away and began to suck. "Kammron, after all, we've done, I owe her a sit-down. Why don't you go downstairs and see what's good with Duke? Tell him I said I appreciate him helping me deliver, Coke."

Kammron mugged Shana. "Shorty, you got twenty minutes, then I'm coming back up here so I can holla at Yasmin. She just had our child, I don't need you up here stressing her out."

Shana felt one emotional shot after the next coming from his lips. Had she been a weaker woman she would have broken down into tears. "That's enough time for me to talk to her, Kammron, thank you."

Kammron took one last look at them, before grabbing his jacket off the couch and slipping it on. He nonchalantly checked the coat for his work and disappeared from the room. As soon as the door closed Shana stepped closer to the bed and looked Coke over. "Girl, you actually finna let that boy name your son, Coke? Don't you know his last name is King?"

Yasmin took Coke off her nipple, and placed him in the bassinet beside her bed, he was passed out. "I know that ain't the reason you came here today, Shana. So, what's really good?"

Shana cleared her throat. "To be honest with you, I was hoping you could tell me. You see the last time we spoke you made it seem like you hated, Kammron. Now y'all are all lovey-dovey and shit, and he's protecting you? What kind of shit is that?" She fought back tears. Yasmin swallowed and readjusted herself on the bed until she was comfortable. Then she exhaled a bunch of air. "Shana, first I wanna let you know, I apologize to you for messing with him. But everything isn't what it seems. To be honest, I don't even know how we got here—me and him I mean."

Shana shook her head angrily. "Seems like you got that conniving shit in your blood to me. Or is it the shit I told you about him turns you on so much you just had to give him some pussy? Ugh, I swear to God, you make me so sick, I don't know what to do. I don't know how I coulda been so stupid. I just figured you were the one person, I could confide in. Turns out you ain't nothing but a snake."

Yasmin nodded her head sympathizing with pain. "You know what, Shana, I deserve everything you're saying. I can see how you can look at me like that, and I'm sorry, so-so sorry. But once again, you need to know things just aren't what they seem. I am still with, Bonkers."

"Oh, bitch puh-lease. That's what makes you so much of a snake. You're actually fucking your nigga's man while he's in a coma. Where the fuck they do that at?" She gave her a look of disgust. "You better hope he never comes out of that coma because the day he does he's going to find out all of your secrets. You forget that Bonkers is just as much of a goon as, Kammron, if not crazier. When that fool finds out you and Kammron been fuckin' around and partying behind his back the entire time he's been in a coma—bitch he gon' cut you into lil' strips and blow that nigga, Kammron off the map. And you know what, you'd deserve it, both of you!"

Yasmin rested her hand on Coke's chest. "Yeah, well, I'll deal with, Bonkers when that time comes. I'm sure he'll be more susceptible to listening to what I have to say than you are. No matter what, when he comes to we're going to be together. I love him contrary to what's taking place with, Kammron."

Shana looked her over in disbelief. "Bitch, you gotta be outta your fuckin' mind. Do you even hear yourself, right now? How the fuck can you possibly love, Bonkers? Or swear that you want to be with him if you can't even keep your legs closed, and hold him down while he's in a fuckin' coma? Damn, bitch, it is real simple. You don't give a fuck about him or nobody else, look what you're doing. You think you finna fuck, Kammron until your man wakes up, then everything is going to be just peachy, really?" She scoffed and laughed. "Not if I have anything to do with it. I promise you, you're going to regret all of this. I been going to see, Bonkers every single day whispering in his ear just praying he wakes up. Oh my God, on the day, he does your ass is grass. Believe that, yours, and Kammron's. Just thought I would let you know."

Kammron opened the door to the hospital room and stepped inside. He mugged Shana. "Bitch, you done in here? I need to make sure she and Coke are straight before I go and handle this bidness tonight."

Shana wanted to say so much. Her feelings were so crushed for how he was acting toward her. She wondered if he'd forgotten they had a small child at home as well? But instead of getting into a huge argument with Kammron, she simply nodded her head.

"Yeah, I'm done, I said all I needed to say." She looked into Yasmin's eyes while saying this, then turned to Kammron. "I guess I'll see you one of these days. I can tell Junior is missing you." She rolled her eyes and stepped into the hallway, closing the door behind her.

Kammron scoffed and mugged the door. "Yo', you good, Goddess? Shorty ain't say shit to get on your nerves, did she?"

Yasmin felt like trash. She glanced over at Coke sleeping soundly in his bassinet and shook her head. "N'all, she was just wishing me well," she lied. "You know how women are." Yasmin was wondering what she had allowed herself to get into. When Bonkers finally did wake up she was really nervous about how things were going to go.

Kammron's phone vibrated with a text from Duke saying they had found the culprits that shot up and ran into one of their traps. Duke was saying a meeting was necessary. He wanted to respond but his phone was clicking on and off due to the lack of reception in the hospital. "Yo,' Goddess, I'll be right back. I gotta go and make a move real quick. I'll see you in a minute." He kissed her on the forehead and headed for the door.

Before he could get to the door, she stopped him. "Kammron, wait! When you get back you and I are going to need to talk. It's very important, please, Kamm." She batted her eyelashes at him.

He smiled and rushed over to kiss her lips. "A'ight baby, anything for you, I'll be back in a minute." Then he was gone.

T.J. Edwards

Chapter 11

Duke loaded a hunnit round magazine into his Mac-90 and cocked it. He had a mug on his face and China White in his system, as he sat in the passenger seat of Kammron's candy apple, red Benz truck sitting on forty-inch rims. It was one o'clock in the morning, on a rainy night. Kammron had his truck parked across the street from People's night club? People's night club was one of the most famous grungy clubs in all of Harlem. It was run by a female named Donna who had mad respect from all of the locals.

Kammron loaded his second Glock, cocked it, and placed it inside his Marc Jacob coat pocket. Kammron was high as a seven-forty-seven Jet. He'd learned how to fight through the dozing off, but the scratching still drove him crazy. He ran his hand over his face before he slid the ski mask over his head.

"Yo', mafuckas gotta be out of their mind to think they can come all the way from Yonkers to run shit? I'm Harlem, mafuckas got the game twisted." He closed his eyes for a second and reopened them.

Duke snickered. "Like I said, these niggas get down for the dirty-dirty, but this is our homeland. Ain't no way in hell we finna let no mafucka come through Harlem on some bully shit. Nickey Barnes wouldn't have allowed this shit. Neither would Resanae." Nickey Barnes and Resanae were Harlem kingpins and legends way before their time. When it came to getting serious money in Harlem those two's names were always mentioned. "Harlem got a new king now, and it's a must you stand on that shit, B. Word to Uptown."

Kammron nodded and sniffed hard. "Watch the God in action. I'm finna put all this shit to rest, you finna see. Come on, Donna said we can roll through the back of the club. We gon' use the separate entrance and see what's really good."

Duke frowned and scratched his head. "Fuck is you using a ski mask for. I thought we was just doing a sit down first?" Kammron smacked his open hand to his forehead. "Damn, Son, I'm bugging." He pulled it off his head and tucked it into his coat pocket. "We ain't gon' need to use these masks until after we come out of here. Come on, bruh, let's make it happen?"

Kammron opened the door to his truck and jogged across the street. The front of the Club was full of cars, and trucks. The parking lot was no better. They ran through the rain, and around to the back of the building. Once there, Kammron took the spare key out of his pants pocket and slid it into the lock. They could hear the music bellowing from the speakers inside the club. There was also the faint scent of sex, and perfume in the air. In addition to People's being a night club, Donna also red-lighted call girls out of the upstairs of the establishment. When Kammron got the door opened he pushed it in and walked smack dead into a huge security guard. Before the security guard could say anything to him, Duke upped a 9mm and placed it to the man's neck.

The security guard held his hands in this air. "Say, man, don't nobody try and rob this club, it belongs to, Ms. Donna, the mother of Harlem."

Donna slid out of the shadows with two Glocks in her hand. One beam fell on Kammron's forehead, the other on Duke's. She was seconds away from deading both of them until she stepped forward and was able to make out Kammron's face. She breathed a sigh of relief. "Whew, boy you're lucky. Kammron, I almost blew your fucking head off." This five-eight, brown-skinned, heavy-set woman told him.

Duke eased the gun from the security guard's neck and trailed his eyes up to the beam that remained on his forehead. He coulda been taken out of the game, he began thanking God for small blessings. "Yo,' Donna get that fuckin' straight line off of my shit. You're making me nervous."

Kammron laughed and walked toward her. When he was in her face, he slid his arms around her frame. "What's really good, Auntie?" He kissed her on both cheeks. She lowered her weapons and put them away. "Been a rash of break-ins all around the community lately. I ain't just talking about the normal run of the mill break-ins, I'm saying they been targeting the respected citizens of our borough. I been in Harlem my whole life, Kammron. Everybody knows me, they know I am the one that keeps this community going. I know deep in my heart those hooligans upstairs has something to do with this. Ever since they came over here from Yonkers things have been all out of whack. Now I know them son of a bitches upstairs are up to no good. You're our last line of defense against these outsiders, go up there and give them hell. Tell them to leave us the fuck alone, or else," she ordered.

****

The stairs squeaked under Kammron's and Duke's feet as they made their way up. Once they made it to the very top the scent of pussy became loud, along with that of cigarette smoke. The hallway had ten rooms that had sheets up. Behind those sheets were working girls, selling the best of Harlem's very own pussy. Each room had its music all the way up. Kammron took the dark hallway to the very end and knocked on the door. Duke carried his Mach-90 in a briefcase. He was ready for whatever. Hoping they could get an understanding with the dudes from Yonkers but not tripping if they couldn't. One way or another he felt things would get figured out.

The door opened, and a short heavy-set dude named Jason stood in the doorway with a blue bandanna around his neck.

Behind him were four other men, and the female that Kammron had tortured a bit. He had on a New York Yankees fitted cap and spoke with a raspy voice that sounded horrible to Kammron.

"Bout time you niggas showed up. The homies was beginning to think we was on a blank mission, step inside." Each member of their crew was already seated at the round table.

Kammron stepped inside and mugged all of them. "First and for most, nigga you don't invite me to come inside nowhere in Harlem. This is my muthafuckin' borough, I invite you inside. I don't know what the fuck you Yonkers niggas on, but ain't shit moving in Uptown. Let's get that shit straight, right now."

Jason laughed. "Oh, nigga you about to find out if we can't get an understanding. I don't give a fuck what you're used to, Harlem is about to open up, and you're finna share North New York. That's just how that's finna work, Kid, word up. Have a seat."

Kammron felt like upping both of his gats and bussing until the clips were empty. He didn't like Jason already. "You got the game fucked up, Dunn. Ain't shit moving, the only reason I agreed to this sit down is so I can see where you're coming from.

Jason sat and clasped his fingers. "Yonkers is in the muthafuckin' building, and I sit at the head. This is my proposal to you. If you allow me and my crew, along with thirty of our entourage to push this first-class base in ten blocks of Harlem, I'll pay a fee to you of a hunnit gees a month for six months. After six months, we can come back to the table and renegotiate this verbal contract." Jason pulled out a cigarette and lit the tip. Almost immediately the scent of the smoke gave Kammron a headache.

Kammron sucked his teeth. "What ten blocks are you talking about, and what is base?"

"You can give us any ten blocks in Harlem as long as they are in the slums. And as far as what base is—" He smiled at his guy P.

P. took a vial from his shirt pocket and rolled it across the table. Kammron picked it up and shook it up and down in his hand. The narcotic was shiny, and the color of crystals, yet at the same time there were specks of yellow inside of it. He took the top off the vial and sniffed lightly. "What the fuck is this?"

"It's something that's about to turn Harlem upside down. I'm talking this finna hit the streets like crack did in the eighties. The best part about it is the world ain't even ready for it. Two thousand and nineteen is the new eighties once this shit hit the streets," Jason jacked. He looked over at P and P smiled back at him.

Kammron passed the vial to Duke. "What exactly is it, and how much does a vial like that go for?"

"That right there is ten dollars, chump change. The contents are a new Yonkers secret, but one thing I can tell you is the high lasts for two hours, and when the teens come down, they come crashing hard. It makes them want to jump off a bridge if they can't go back upwards." Jason smiled. He held the vial in his fingers. "This ain't like that North Korean shit, it's worse. Physically a person ain't got no other choice than to stay under the spell every day all day, or it's a wrap." He stared across at Kammron.

Kammron continued to look over the vial. He took the contents and poured it on the table. Then pulled a Swiss Army knife out of his pocket and chopped through it. It felt crunchy and smelled like wax. He couldn't decipher the contents, but he figured if he was able to get a nice portion in front of Zeek, Zeek could look it over and tell him exactly what was inside.

Zeek was his chemist and was a legend in Harlem for being a cook in that trap house kitchen. He could take any measure of work and turn it into three times itself. He was a beast. Kammron scooped the crumbs back into the vial. When the majority of it was back in, he touched the tip of his tongue and felt it go numb. He didn't like the feeling.

Jason leaned over the table. "A hunnit gees a month, for six months. You can't beat that, Kammron, and neither could ya mans, right here."

"And after six months if I want you muthafuckas out. Then what's gon' happen?" Kammron asked, looking over the room full of Yonkers Hittas.

Jason sat back in his seat and clasped his fingers together. "I don't think that's something you gonna wanna do. I think Harlem is big enough for all of us. Long as everybody eating and doing what they supposed to be doing it shouldn't be a problem.

"That's not answering my question. And Harlem is only big enough for me and my day-ones. Not you, niggas from Yonkers. Why y'all ain't trying to push that shit out there?" Kammron asked he felt himself getting increasingly irritated with how cocky Jason was acting. He was seconds away from splashing him and his crew.

Jason held up his hands. "Look bruh, Harlem is your world. All me and my dudes asking is for a six-month run. If you can give us that then whatever you say at the end is law? You want us to move around then it's cool. We'll take our troops, and that New Yonkers back to our homeland immediately, you got my word on that." He sneered at Kammron, with no intentions on fulfilling his word. All he wanted was a footstep inside Harlem. He knew once he got going, he was going to be able to conquer the entire borough. North New York was his.

Kammron looked him over. There was no way he could pass up six hundred thousand dollars. It didn't matter if came in six months, or an entire year. Most people didn't make six hundred thousand dollars in an entire year. He wasn't worried about the Yonkers boys doing more than he allowed them to do. If worst came to worst, he could always send those Hittas at them to wipe them off the face of Harlem for good. Kammron liked the sound of that. He couldn't help but be a little greedy, and a little grimy.

"Yo', when I'ma get my first payment?"

Jason snickered. "As soon as you give us our post. Anything across Frederick Douglas Boulevard a be one hunnit."

Kammron nodded. "A'ight, I'ma fuck wit' you niggas, but all that other bullshit gotta stop. I don't know who been hitting up our respected local spots, breaking into them, and doing all of that shit, but it's gotta be you, new niggas. That shit gotta cease to exist. Get your animals in order or the Gods gon' have to put they ass down. Word to Uptown."

Jason nodded his head. "That's the least I can do after you accepting me into your borough. Put the word out to the rest of Harlem. That way we won't have to be warring wit' every Harlem nigga in town. I'll do my part, you got my word on that." Jason stood up and extended his hand.

Kammron shook it very briefly, before leaving the room. He took one last look at the girl he'd caused so much pain before he left the room beside Duke. She had her nose all bandaged up. He didn't feel a twinge of remorse.

T.J. Edwards

Chapter 12

Two weeks into their approval, the crew from Yonkers hit the game hard. Kammron had given them ten blocks along St. Nicholas. A short distance away from the Harlem River Houses, they took it and ran. On each block, they had teens lined up as if they were in Disney Land waiting to get on a famous ride. Other blocks that Kammron had given them had traffic jams, with a few teens from Harlem running up and down the cars serving them the product Jason and his crew had brought from Yonkers. They called the drug Magic because it gave the fiends the feeling of being high off meth, crack, and China at the same time.

The high lasted for two and a half hours, and end result over the user came crashing hard, then their body began to immediately fiend for the drug. It gave them cramps and made them feel sick on the stomach. It caused the person to become both physically and psychologically dependent on the narcotic. In the game, a product like that was guaranteed to get a dope boy filthy rich.

In the third week, Duke pulled up on Kammron in a pecan Jaguar, sitting on triple cheese Forgiatos. He lowered his tinted windows, as Kammron was just about to get into his cherry Range Rover. "Yo', Kid, we gotta talk numbers. I think we made a mistake, come fuck wit' me."

Kammron grabbed his .40 from under his driver's seat and tucked it back into his waistband. He closed the door to his truck and walked down to Duke's Jag. He jumped into the passenger seat after nodding at the security detail that was parked behind Duke inside of a black Chevy Astro van. Kammron knew they were heavily armed on the inside. He'd arranged for one of the females from Harlem with a license, and no record to drive his hittas around. In fact, all of his security was rolling that way. As soon as Kammron got into the car Duke pulled from the curb. Snow began to fall from the sky in large thickets. Kammron adjusted himself in his seat. There were two Harlem shooters in the back seat of Duke's whip with fully automatics on their laps, and black shades on their faces. They surveyed the entire area of whence they drove.

"So, what's good, Duke?"

"Say, Kid, our sales are down. Ever since the city done got wind of this Magic shit, they been chasing that dope just like everybody else. Mafuckas is converting left and right. If we don't find a solution soon, we gon' be fucked in the game. I mean that."

Kammron frowned and watched the snow began to come down heavier. "When you say sales are down, explain that to me because you just picked up a bag of money that seemed about right to me for our weekly average."

Duke bent a corner and continue to cruise. "That bag you got is about a hunnit gees short of what it was three weeks ago at this time. A lot of our customers are rejecting the China man, they are over there across St. Nicholas laying up in Jason's needle houses man. That poison them niggas pushing is taking over the game. I think us allowing them into Harlem was a bad idea."

Kammron sat in silence for a second and pulled the hairs on his chin. He was feeling some type of way about Duke's statement because he knew Duke was saying Kammron had made a bad decision allowing Jason and his Yonkers crew inside of Harlem. Duke had a way of saying things without actually coming right out and saying them.

"I found out that them bitch niggas been running that sake gambit all up and down the East Coast? They got some of their men in Virginia, Philly, D.C., the Carolinas, and Baltimore doing the same damn thing, and pushing the same damn product. Them mafuckas making a killing, and now we done gave them a key to New York through Harlem. There is only one solution for us to get back on track before things go south," Duke said, turning another corner.

Kammron continued to look out of the window. "Oh yeah, well what's that?"

"We gotta jump on ship, and cop some of that shit they pushing. It seems like it's the new wave of the world. You already know everything starts in New York before it goes anywhere else. I think that Magic shit is going to be the truth in the next few years. It's the new crack, there are millions to be made off that shit, and they the only ones cashing out, right now. That ain't how that's finna stay."

Kammron listened with a trained ear. He understood where Duke was going with things, and he liked the lane he was driving in. "Say, Dunn, you already know I take your advice like a verse from the Bible. I'm rocking wit' you one hunnit percent. If you thinking we need to cop some of that Magic, then that's what we gon' do. Hit up Jason and see what he wanna do. Get me the numbers and I'll get you the cash. Sound like a deal to you?"

Duke nodded. "That's official, I'll do just that and fuck wit' you in a minute. Oh, before I forget, we been having a lil' trouble with a few of our spots being ran into. It seems like we got a few lone wolves out there that insist on testing our establishment. I'm getting to the bottom of it, right now. As soon as I do you'll know what's good because we're going to move accordingly." Duke pulled back in front of Kammron's house and threw the car in park. "I just wanted to give you an update in person. You know the Feds is watching. A mafucka can never be too careful." He shook up with Kammron and gave him half of a hug.

Kammron patted his back and broke the embrace. "Do what you gotta do nigga. I think I'ma take me a few days off just to breathe. When I get my head clear, I'ma hit you up and we gon' handle this bidness. As soon as you get them numbers from Jason let me know what's really good." Kammron bumped fists with the killas in the back seat of Duke's whip, before he got out, and Duke stormed away from the front of the house with his security detail following him.

****

Duke eased into the hot tub and sank all the way down until the water covered his chest. He drank from a bottle of Moët, taking one guzzle after the next. He could barely keep his eyes open. He had a hundred thousand-dollars-worth of Jewelry around his neck, and Cartier lenses on his face. "Baby, what's taking you so long? Bring yo lil' thick ass in here so I can see what you looking like."

Shana slowly stepped into the room wearing a one-piece Burberry bikini. She did a slow circle and allowed Duke to take in all of her thickness. She especially wanted him to see how the front of the material cuffed her pussy. Shana was strapped and she knew it. When she was facing him, she licked her juicy glossy lips.

"Well, what do you think, baby?" She stepped closer to the hot tub.

As soon as she was close enough, Duke slid his hand between Shana's thick thighs and rubbed her pussy. The material had already slipped between the folds of her sex. It felt hot and squishy. Duke smushed her sex lips together and felt his piece harden. "Ma, you look sexy as hell. I fuck wit' Killa the long way, and I still can't understand how he could kick you to the curb. A woman as fine as you deserve to be put up on a pedestal. Word up."

Shana shivered, she had never heard any man talk about her in the ways Duke always did. He made her feel so good. It was one of the many reasons she didn't mind sleeping around with him behind Kammron's back. She didn't know how Kammron was going to act when he found out about them and she didn't even care. As far as she was concerned, he was doing his thing with Yasmin, and she was doing hers with Duke. She didn't owe him any explanation. She hated men who felt they had a stake on a woman just because they had a child with her. In her mind, it wasn't how the game was supposed to go, especially when you had a baby daddy like Kammron.

Duke cuffed her ass and pulled her to him. He sucked all over her neck and licked her earlobe. "I want you so bad, right now, Shana. I been thinking about you all day long. Am I crazy for that?"

Shana moaned and shook her head. "N'all, I been thinking about you, too." She lifted her foot and sat it on the rim of the hot tub, allowing Duke to continue to rub her pussy. Her eyes rolled to the back of her head when he pulled the crotch to the side and slid two fingers into her warmth. Her pussy was already dripping wet. He fingered her for a full minute, pulled his fingers out, and sucked them into his mouth. He licked all between the cracks of them. Shana moved in and kissed his lips, sucking her juices from his lips. Her tongue traced all over them.

Duke stood up with his dick poking against her stomach. She stepped inside of the hot tub and bent over, looking back at him.

"Come on, baby. You already know I love the way you strip me down." She could feel her pussy quivering.

Duke grabbed her shoulder straps and yanked them down her shoulders, down her waist, all the way until her chocolate pussy was exposed to the air. As soon as he saw it, he began to tremble. He smacked the side of her right cheek and watched it jiggle then rubbed her ass.

"You think you ready for me, Shana, huh?" He got behind her and lined himself up. His head slowly eased between her lips.

Shana arched her back and slammed backward to receive all of him. "Uhhhh!" She grabbed the side of the hot tub and used it to push back against him as hard as she could. "Yes-yes-yes!"

Duke held her hips and felt extreme pleasure as she worked him hungrily. He raised his hand high into the air and brought it down onto her backside, before fucking her as fast, and as hard as he could. Shana drove him mad, there was something about her, he couldn't get enough of. He was still looking for the right opportunity to let Kammron know how he felt about her, but in his mind, there hadn't been an appropriate opportunity for him to do so.

He didn't think Kammron would have a problem with it, especially because he spent most of his time worrying about Yasmin. In Duke's mind even if Kammron did have a problem with him and Shana fuckin' around Kammron didn't have any legs to stand on because Duke felt the same thing he was doing to Kammron, Kammron was doing it to Bonkers. It was Harlem, nobody's bitch was really their bitch as far as he was concerned.

He pumped into Shana as hard as he could. He loved her shiny dark-skin. He still couldn't believe she was Puerto Rican and so dark at the same time. He grabbed a handful of her hair and pulled on it. She shrieked and fucked backward into him even harder. Her breasts bounced up and down, the nipples were rock hard. Duke kept his eyes pinned on their connection. He liked watching himself slide in and out of Shana's box.

"Mmm-mmm-mmm-mmm!"

Shana closed her eyes tightly and thought back to the days when she was only a little girl and she used to see Duke walking up a down the street with his shirt off. She remembered it doing something to her even back then. The image of him in her mind made her pussy just a tad bit wetter. When she thought about the fact that she was fucking Kammron's right-hand man at the moment, it caused her to cum as she moaned at the top of her lungs.

"Uh! Uh! Uh, Duke—ohhh, Duke!" she hollered.

Duke speeded up and came back to back. After he finished, Shana stood up and wrapped her arms around his neck kissing his lips. "I'm so glad you're in my life, Duke. You make me feel so good, I just want to let you know I am yours. I'ma ride for you Duke, just mark my words."

Duke wrapped his arms around her body and held her after kissing her forehead. "I got you, too, boo. Word is bond, I got you."

T.J. Edwards

Chapter 13

Kammron sat back on the couch inside of Bonkers' hospital room and watched as Yasmin fixed the sheets that were over Bonkers. She smoothed them out and stopped to rub his cheek. Her face had turned a shade red. Her eyes watered and then tears sailed down her cheeks. She wiped them away and laid her face beside Bonkers'. "I miss you so much, Bonkers. I know you're in there, baby. I need you to come out because I need you, and I love you. Yazzy needs you, and Yazzy loves you as well. These last few months have been crazy without you. They've been tough, but just like I am begging you to fight forward, I am trying to do the same. I just love you so much." She dropped her head and started sobbing.

Kammron sat on the couch both irritated, and annoyed. He couldn't believe how Yasmin was carrying on after everything he'd been doing for her ever since Bonkers had been down. A selfish part of him wanted her to forget all about Bonkers. He felt he had put in more than enough work for her to have done so.

"Yo', Yasmin quit all that mafuckin' crying and shit. That ain't gon' make bruh come to no faster." He frowned and stood up.

Yasmin wiped her face clean of tears. "I know, Kammron but I just miss him so much. It seems like he's not getting any better and having him here is costing us a fortune. I just don't know what to do." She rested her head on his chest.

Kammron scoffed. "Aaahhh, so now it's *us*? Just a few minutes ago you wasn't hollerin' that is shit. You was too busy being all up that nigga's ass. You was making it seem like I ain't been on shit since the homie been down. Pissed me the fuck off." He was heated.

Yasmin shook her head. "I'm sorry, Kammron, I didn't mean it like that. You have to know, I appreciate everything you have done for me, and Yazzy ever since he's been down. You have been an incredible man in every sense of the word. I mean that."

Kammron smacked his lips. "Well, you definitely ain't actin' like it, but it's all good. This shit ain't about me, right now. I see where your heart is, and I ain't finna keep trying to stand in the way of what you and Bonkers got going on. Matter fact from here on out, I'm just gon' let you do you." Kammron grabbed his jacket off the couch and got ready to leave out of the hospital room when Yasmin blocked his path. Kammron mugged her. "Yasmin, get the fuck out of my way, I'm serious."

"Kammron, why does of have to be like this? Why must we fight for no reason? I mean you already know what it is when it comes to, me and Bonkers. You said you were cool with our arrangement. Now all of a sudden you're acting brand new."

Kammron grabbed her by the arm and pulled her out of the way. "Bitch stop playin' wit' me. Ain't no mafucka acting brand new. Shit just didn't dawn on me until I heard how much love and care you got for this, nigga. Ain't no reason for me continuing to try and do the most for yo' ass when your heart is all wrapped up in, bruh. So, I'm done, I couldn't care less what y'all do from here on out."

Yasmin pushed him as hard as she could making him stumble away from the door. "Muthafucka you not finna do to me what you did to, Shana. I just had your whole ass baby. You owe me more than what you been giving me. I ain't accepting nothing less than that. You gon' have to whoop my ass every single day or kill me before you to kick me to the curb," Yasmin threatened feeling her heart pounding in her chest. Kammron had caught his balance and was staring at Yasmin with penetrating anger. He stepped into her face and backhanded her without even thinking about it. She fell to one knee, holding her face. "Bitch don't you ever put your hands on a God. Fuck is wrong wit' you?" he snarled.

Yasmin slowly stood up and balled her fists. "Nigga, you think I'm scared of you, Kammron?" She stepped into his face again. She could feel her face stinging where he had slapped the living daylights out of her. She swung and hit him so hard he bit his tongue. "Don't you ever slap me again, Kammron. I'm not afraid of you, you gon' respect me. I am the mother of your son."

Kammron used the tip of his finger to dab at the blood coming out of his tongue. He looked it over and laughed, then turned the lock on the hospital room door and pulled his .357 revolver out of his coat pocket. "So, you think you got enough heart to come at me now, huh? A mafucka been hitting that pussy on a regular. So, you thinking it's sweet, not knowing I'm the muthafuckin' king of Harlem. A'ight, since you acting like you got a death wish." He opened the cylinder of his .357 and dropped all six bullets into the palm of his hand. Then he replaced one bullet into the chamber, spun it and clicked it closed, then aimed the gun at her. "Come here, bitch!"

Yasmin felt like her heart literally skipped a beat. She swallowed her spit, and slowly made her way over to him. "Kammron, what the hell are you doing?" She held her hands at shoulder level.

Kammron curled his upper lip, cocked the hammer on the gun, and tightened his grip. "Bitch you think you got a death wish, right?"

Yasmin shook her head. "I never said anything about dying. How could I possibly think of being that negligent when I got two children to think about? They need me here, and so does, Bonkers."

Kammron was just about to lower his gun until she'd said the last part. As soon as those words rolled off her tongue he aimed the gun at her forehead and pulled the trigger.

Click!

Yasmin jumped backward and closed her eyes. She expected a bullet to fire out of his gun and slam into her. When it didn't, she began to shake, and tremble. "Kammron, I'm sorry, please put that gun away! I didn't mean to put my hands on you. Let's just go back to the way it was. You and I can continue to exist together as long as Bonkers is in this state. You've done an amazing job this far, and I really appreciate you."

Kammron waved her off. "Fuck that." He opened the cylinder, spun it, slammed it back in place and pressed the barrel to his temple before pulling the trigger again.

Click!

He closed his eyes and pulled it again.

Click!

"Aahhh, that shit feels so good, don't it?"

Yasmin backed up and shook her head. "No, Kammron, you're sick, this isn't normal." She backed up so far she bumped into Bonkers' bed. She saw Kammron was still walking forward with his gun in hand. She began to panic.

Kammron didn't stop until the barrel was pressed against her chin again. He cocked the hammer. "See Yasmin, you really don't have the slightest idea of who you're fucking with. I been real sweet wit' yo' ass, but that ain't me. You dealing with a muthafuckin' Harlem monster," he threatened, barely above a whisper, pulling the trigger three quick times.

Yasmin fell to her knees. "Please Kammron, you're going to give me a heart attack."

Kammron busted out laughing. He grabbed her by her hair and kissed her lips. "Bitch you and Bonkers deserve each other. I could never love you the way he do. That shit just ain't in me. So, y'all do y'all, and I'ma do me." He cuffed her ass and licked her neck. "I'll see you when I see you." He replaced his gun and disappeared from the room.

As soon as he was gone, Yasmin fell to her knees and broke into a fit of tears. She was so tired of it all. The lifestyle, Kammron, Bonkers being in a coma, being a mother, having to worry about her safety every second of every day. It was all becoming too exhausting. She remained on her knees and tilted her head to the sky. "Father in the mighty name of Jesus I ask that you hear my prayers. Please give me the strength, and the determination to press forward. Help me to make it through another day because I am growing so weak. I am losing my will to fight. Father I need you, I need you to give me a sign everything is going to be alright. Show me a portion of your light, please. In Jesus Holy and precious name, I beg of you." She bowed her head and remained planted that way as more tears rolled down her cheeks.

"Ahhh! Ahhh! Ahhh!" Bonkers hollered sitting up in bed, after pulling the breathing tube out of his mouth.

Yasmin nearly jumped out of her skin. She rushed to his side. "Help! Help! I need a nurse, I need a nurse, fast! My man is awake!" she screamed.

****

Kammron knocked on Stacie's door for the third time and finally saw the lights turn on inside the front room. Stacie peeked out of the front window and answered the door. She opened it and placed her hand on her hip. "Kammron, why are you beating on my door like you're the fuckin' Feds?"

Kammron brushed past her. "First of all, the Feds don't beat on doors. They knock them, bitches, down, and second of all, I'm in need of some motherly affection, I'm stressing." He stepped into her living room and kicked his Timbs off.

Stacie closed the door and placed her finger to her lips. "Shush boy, I just put Junior to sleep, and my male friend is back there. I don't know what you're going through but it's going to have to wait until the morning." She looked over her shoulder, down the long hallway that led to her room.

Kammron looked her up and down. He peeped the way her short negligée barely fell below her ass. He could see the bottom portions of her cheeks. The sight ignited a hunger within him. He jumped up, and stepped into her face, pulling her into his embrace. "Who the fuck you got back there? He ain't no made nigga like me," Kammron jacked.

Stacie fought her way out of his grasp and backed away from him. "Kammron, who I got back in my room is my business. Your business is Shana, and Kamm Jr, not me. Can you dig that?"

"*Can I what?*" Kammron frowned and yanked her back to him. "Stacie you live in Harlem. I run Harlem, and I own every bitch in this mafucka. So, I don't care who you got back there. That nigga can push on or meet this mafucka, right here." He pulled a .40 Glock from the small of his back and cocked it. He was high as a kite and wasn't thinking logically.

Stacie shivered into his body from fear. "Okay, Kammron, calm down. Just tell mama what's the matter?" She figured if she referred to herself as a person he was supposed to protect she would have a better chance of him listening to her, and no one getting hurt. Kammron had a lethal temper that she was more than aware of. The last thing she wanted was for Kammron to lose his cool and do something stupid.

"I'm here for you, baby. I mean that with every fiber of my being."

Kammron became a bit calmer. "Now that's more like it." He replaced the gun and rubbed all over her exposed cheeks. Then slipped his fingers up under her negligée to feel that she was without panties. "Damn, ma, I see you was planning on getting a lil' action, huh?" His fingers delved into her folds and found warmth and wetness.

Stacie cringed and held his shoulders. "Kammron, we definitely can't do nothing like this. My man is in the other room, and I care about him. I'm trying to turn over a new leaf." She extended her hands and tried to push Kammron off her. "Please Kammron."

Kammron held her tighter and sucked on her neck. "You think I give a fuck about that other, nigga? I said I need some motherly affection, right now. You can either give me that, or I'm finna go back there and splash that nigga. His blood gon' be on your hands, and I ain't gon' give a fuck."

Stacie felt as if she was caught between a rock and a hard place. "Listen to me, Kammron, he sleep. I'm here for you, just tell me what you need. What can mama do for you, baby?"

Kammron softened and hugged her. "I'm just tired ma, I feel like the streets starting to fuck with my head. I can handle the shit, but the process is just crazy." He sniffed and pulled on his nose. Then hugged Stacie tighter.

Stacie rubbed his back. "Baby, so what do you need from me most specifically?"

Kammron cuffed that ass. "On some real shit, I need you to give me some of this body. I wanna fuck this pussy, right now." He rubbed the front of her panties and cuffed her naked pussy. The feel of her heat made him shudder.

Stacie wanted to tell him no, she wanted to tell him to get out of her house, but instead, she pulled him into the spare room and dropped to her knees.

Chapter 14

Kammron thrusted himself in and out of Stacie's mouth. He felt the way Stacie's tongue wrapped around his dick. It drove him crazy. "Damn ma, make me feel better. Fuck—make ya mans feel better."

Stacie gripped him harder in her hand. She stroked him back and forth and sucked as hard as she could. She popped her mouth off him and continued to stroke him. "You ready for some of this pussy, baby? You ready for mama to put this box on yo' lil' ass?"

Kammron's dick was jumping up and down. He was fiending for some of her pussy now, he needed that overgrown cat. It was the only way he would feel better. "Hell, yeah ma, I'm ready, right now. Get yo' ass up here and let me handle this bidness."

Stacie stood up and bent over the bed. She pulled the neg-ligée all the way up to her waist and smacked her naked ass. "Come on lil', Daddy, fuck Mama. It's all good!"

Kammron started shaking as he slid deep into her sex. "Uhhhh, Stacie, tell your baby boy to fuck this pussy." He slammed inside and worked her over at full speed. "Tell me, Stacie, I wanna hear that shit!" he growled.

Stacie balled the comforter in her hand and spread her thighs apart. "Yes-yes-unnhh, baby boy, fuck this pussy! Fuck this pussy—Mama needs that," she moaned playing along with his fantasy.

Kammron shivered again and went to work. He started fucking her with all his might. Long stroking her wet pussy that felt better than all the rest. Kammron had always preferred the sex of an older woman to that of a girl his age. In his opin-ion fuck sessions with women above thirty always went better, and he was able to release more of his pent-up frustrations with them. He had always fantasized about Stacie as a kid. Now that he was able to fuck her it still was surreal to him. He speeded up his pace and proceeded to go bananas inside of her.

Stacie flipped her long hair over her face and bit into the bed before she screamed at the top of her lungs because he was dicking her down. She felt him reach between her thighs, then he was diddling her clit sending quivers through her body. She shook, came hard and landed on the bed with him still pumping full speed behind her.

Kammron sucked his middle finger and slid it into her backdoor, then sawed it in and out of her rapidly. "I—want—some—of—this—ass—Stacie!" He pulled his dick out of her pussy and rested it on her rosebud. It was dripping and heavily oiled with her juices. He eased into her hole and forced his pipe inside. "Staci—cee—"

Her anal ring squeezed him for dear life. She gritted her teeth and sighed as he filled her up. She scratched at the bed, she felt Kammron pull all the way out, then he slammed forward as hard as he could. He pulled back out and repeated the process. In a matter of seconds, he was fucking her ass at full speed while holding her slim waist.

Clap! Clap! Clap! Clap! Was the sounds of their skin smacking into each other.

Kammron stayed on her for a full twenty minutes before he came hard, landing on top of her. They wound up on the bed a few minutes later. Stacie crawled up it and rested her hand on Kammron's chest. "Baby, is that all that you needed from me?" She kissed his left nipple. She was hoping it was because she needed to get him out of the house before her man came out of the bedroom.

Kammron yawned and nodded. "Yeah, I'm finna get the fuck out of here. I appreciate you ma, that was all I needed." He slapped her on the ass, got dressed and bounced.

****

Later that night, Duke caught Kammron before he pulled into the driveway of his home. He jumped out of his truck and met him. Kammron stepped out with a look of irritation. It was just beginning to snow. "Yo', what's good, Kid? Fuck you doing out here this late at night?"

"It's them Yonkers niggas, Kamm. Son, they ain't acting right." He looked over his shoulder to see where their Hittas were stationed.

Kammron waved for Duke to follow him. "Yo', let's head inside of my pad. We need to talk, and you need to put me up on game. So, I can know what's really taking place in Harlem."

Duke followed him upstairs and was on his way inside of the house but first, he turned around and gave the orders to his men to be on high alert. Then he stepped inside and locked the door behind him.

Kammron staggered to the couch and plopped down on it. "Fuck going on, Duke? I can already tell you got some shit on your mind, fill me in."

Duke sat on the couch across from Kammron, took a package of raw out of his pocket and poured out some of the powder on Kammron's glass table before he tooted four thin lines of it. Once the drug was coursing through his veins, he felt breezy. His eyes became heavy, and his brain seemed to compute things a lot better.

"Kid, it turns out of that Magic shit they pushing is actually a fuckin' gold mine. Kid, new making around a million dollars a day, and that's just by use of the ten blocks that we gave them across the way. I think we settled out for that hunnit thousand a month a little too soon." Duke shook his head and closed his eyes.

Kammron sat up, listening attentively. He could see Duke was high as a kite. It made his stomach hurt, then all of a sudden his body began to crave the China White. He felt a cramp shoot through him. "So, what you think we should be doing, Duke?"

"Nigga, I ain't even got to the best part yet." Duke sat up as best he could and opened his eyes. He looked right across the living room at Kammron. "Yo', Son, it turns out them Yonkers niggas just picked up a contract from Showbiz for Jimmy's head, first, then yours. Kid, nem set to make a million off each hit, and for a bonus, the Vegas promised them half of Harlem. They will receive their blocks as soon as the coroner signs your death certificate. Another thing, Son nem been bringing more of their troops into Harlem from Yonkers. I think they trying to mount up. I say we start to pick them off as fast as we can before we become the targets. What you think?"

Kammron hopped up, he was boiling mad. "You mean to tell me that these fuck niggas finna try and bite the hands that feed them? They finna try and come at Harlem? Try and take the Don off his throne before the seat even mold to my ass?"

Duke laughed and wiped his nose. "Yo', I knew from the beginning we couldn't trust them, niggas. Son nem even look grimy as a muthafucka. But they most definitely fuckin' wit' the right ones. It's about time we get down for the get down. You feel me?"

Kammron was so heated he was pacing back and forth. He clenched and unclenched his fists. "Yo', on my word, Kid, I wanna fuck these niggas over in an ugly way. I'm talking no mercy, sadistic as it can get type shit. We allowed them to come into Harlem, and eat off our homeland, and this how we are repaid? N'all Son, I can't let this shit ride. I don't give a fuck what they do to Jimmy long as they don't bring that shit over here."

Duke grunted. "It's a lil' too late for that, Kammron. They see you as a threat just as much as, Jimmy. Money talks, Yonkers is set to make two million dollars off your hit, and gain half of Harlem. If they are making a million dollars a day off ten blocks pushing that Magic shit nigga imagine what they finna make with half of Harlem."

"Them niggas ain't finna make one red cent if, Killa Kamm got anything to say about it. They gotta be out of their fuckin' mind. Fuck they think it's sweet or something?" Kammron continued to pace. He was so angry he started sweating. He mugged Duke. "When did you find out this information?"

Duke nodded out and lowered his head into his lap. His eye had become way too heavy for him to keep them open. Kammron allowed him to snore for a second, then clapped his hands as hard as he could to jar him awake. Duke jumped and wiped his face with his hand.

"Found that shit out about three hours ago, but I been watching them, niggas, ever since you gave them the green light into our borough. I already know you can't trust them, sons of bitches, as far as you throw them." His eyes closed again, and then he was snoring.

Kammron nodded and slammed his fist into his hand as hard as he could. "These fuck niggas wanna play wit' me?"

There were footsteps headed up his stairs, then Shana was sliding her key into the lock of the door. When she came in and saw Duke sitting on the couch nodding out, with China residue on the table in front of him, she felt disappointed.

Her eyes went over to Kammron. "Hey?"

Kammron frowned and looked over his Rolex that was flooded in lemon diamonds. "Fuck is you doing coming into the house this late at night? Where are you coming from?"

Shana took her key out of the lock and felt like ignoring him. After all, he had some nerve questioning her. "I stopped by my mother's for a little while but I couldn't stay there because she got company over there. But then again, she said you had left, right before I got there. You care to explain why you were over there?"

Kammron smacked his lips. "Bitch please, you know better than to question the God. Take yo' ass back there and jump in the shower. When you done run me some bathwater. I wanna relax for a lil' minute."

Shana stood there looking at him as if he were crazy. "Are you fuckin' kidding me? You haven't been home in only God knows how long. You been shacked up with another bitch and you think I'm finna come home tired, and run yo bathwater like everything is just peachy? Nigga, you got another think coming. If you want your bath water run then you better get up and go and do that shit yourself. Or you better have, Yasmin, do that shit!" She rolled her eyes and eyed Duke one final time before leaving the living room.

Kammron was in front of her in a heartbeat. "Fuck is wrong wit' you hoes today, huh? Do I got pussy written on my forehead or something?" He glared into her eyes with hatred.

Shana refused to break eye contact. "Kammron, you being pussy ain't got nothing to do with it. It ain't my place to run yo bathwater. You ain't my nigga no more, Duke is." She crossed her arms in front of her chest.

Kammron thought he was hearing things. He turned his head sideways and cupped his ear. "What the fuck did you say?"

Shana took a step back. "You heard me, I'm fucking wit' Duke now. That's Daddy, so if I'm gone run anybody's bathwater, it's going to be his." She looked him up and down challenging.

Kammron snapped. "Bitch, I know you playin' wit' me. I know you're jerking my chain?" He grabbed her by the jacket and tossed her into the living room.

He kicked Duke's Timbs, Duke was snoring loud and boisterously, before Kammron caused him to jump up and pull out his gun. When he saw that it was Kammron he lowered it.

"Damn, Kammron, what the fuck is going on?" His eyes trailed over to Shana. He watched her struggle to get up from the floor.

"Tell him, Duke," Shana cried.

Duke looked surprised. "Tell him what?"

Shana wiped her tears from her face. "Tell him about us, I'm tired of keeping this secret. Maybe if he knew he wouldn't treat me the way he does." Now her tears were dripping off her chin.

Kammron stepped into Duke's face. "Is this true, Duke? You fuckin' with my son's mother behind my back?"

Duke lowered his head, then slowly looked over to Shana. "Bruh, I don't know how to explain what happened between her and me, it just happened. Yeah, I'm fuckin' with her, but I ain't think it'll be a problem seeing as you're fuckin' wit', Yasmin. I ain't even think—"

Smack!

Kammron hit him so hard he went flying backward, and into the glass table. Little specks of glass hopped up into the air and littered the floor. Duke's ass was stuck inside of the frame. Kammron picked him up by his Avirex leather jacket and smacked him again. This time Duke fell on the couch. He sat there for a minute and hopped back up.

Shana rushed over to separate the men. "Hey, stop this, Kammron. You ain't got no right to do what you're doing. Me and you aren't together. All we have is a child together."

Kammron grabbed her by the throat and threw her out of the way. "Shut the fuck up, bitch! This ain't got shit to do with you no more." He stepped back toward Duke. "Fuck nigga, this how you hone do me, huh? You ain't no better than them Yonkers niggas." He raised his hand to smack Duke like a broad again.

Duke smacked Kammron's hand away and punched him as hard as he could sending him flying backward into the wall. He tucked his gun away, and rushed Kammron, tackling him into the wall. "That—shit—wasn't—even—like that." He punched him in the ribs, as they began to tussle, and fell into the hallway that led into the living room.

Kammron struggled against him, blood rushed out of his nose, and into his mouth preventing him from being able to breathe the way he needed to. He felt winded and weak. Duke held him down. Kammron twisted this way and that. He wanted to break free. He had plans of putting a slug inside of Duke's face. There was no way he could let him get away with punching him. He was the king of Harlem. Nickey Barnes would have never accepted such treason.

"Get the fuck off me, nigga."

"Please y'all, just stop this. There is no need to be fighting. Kammron, I'm sorry, I didn't think it was a problem," Shana cried, feeling she had made the worse mistake of her young life by telling Kammron.

Duke continued to hold Kammron down. He knew he had fucked up. He didn't see where they could take things from there. Not only had he caused Kammron to shed blood, but he had done it in front of Shana. He was certain no good could come from their dispute.

"Listen, Kamm, Kid I fucked up. Let's get past this shit, we can't fall out over a woman. I got too much love for you Dunn, word up."

Kammron felt his blood sailing along his neck. He swallowed some of it that was in his mouth. "Yo', just let me up, Dunn. Get the fuck off me!" he ordered.

Duke looked him over closely for a moment, then said fuck it. He hopped up and backed away from Kammron. His high was completely blown. He bucked his eyes and tried to gather himself. "Look, Killa, we gotta let this shit go, bruh. It ain't like y'all was together or nothin'. Had that been the case I would have never pursued her."

Kammron wiped the blood from his nose and smeared it across his Gucci jeans. He swallowed his bloody spit and started laughing. "You know what, I'm tripping." He looked over at Shana. "This bitch ain't worth all of that. Fuck I look like getting at my mans when it's her I should be checking, and even so a nigga can't turn a ho into a housewife anyway, right?"

Shana felt offended. "Kammron, I ain't a ho, and you know I'm not. Duke is only the second man I've ever been with, and hopefully the last." She stepped next to Duke.

"Yo', Kid, I apologize, Dunn. I swear on the borough I ain't never mean to cross you. Or do anything behind your back like a snake. Me and shorty just sort of happened. It ain't got shit to do with my love and loyalty for you. That's on my mother."

Kammron shook his head and smiled. "Yo', it's good, you're Duke-Da-God, right?"

Duke stared at him trying to see where he was going with this question. "Right."

Kammron extended his hand. "To that new nigga wit' my old ho, kudos."

Duke hesitated and very slowly shook his hand. "O-kay, so does this mean we're cool?"

Kammron nodded. "As a fan, besides we got some major shit to take care of anyway, right? Ain't no sense in me beefing over pussy I done already had. Y'all good, I wish you the best." Kammron slapped Duke on the shoulder and leaned into his ear but spoke loud enough for Shana to hear it. "Get that bitch out my crib and don't ever bring her around me again. She is right, now, and forever your responsibility. You dig that?"

Duke nodded and looked Kammron over from the corner of his eyes. "Yeah, a'ight."

Kammron smiled. "Y'all get the fuck out my house. Duke we on bidness first thang in the morning."

Chapter 15

Kammron popped his black hoodie over his head and knocked on the third door in the hallway. Duke waited on the side of the door with a twelve-gauge shotgun in his hands, and a ski mask covering his face. It was three days later, and Kammron was finally setting up an operation to *Move them Yonkers niggas around, in motion.* He'd gotten a tip from one of his loyal users that four of Jason's hittas were staying at an apartment complex right across the street from Ruckers Park. The apartment was not only a place where the shooters laid their heads, but they also pushed some of the Magic out of the spot. This was why Kammron now knocked on the door in the guise of a user. He hugged himself and balanced his weight from one foot, and on to the other.

One of the shooters peeked out of the peephole. He saw a hooded Kammron with his head down and figured he was there to purchase some work. He opened the door with the chain still attached to it.

"Fucks really good, my nigga, what you want?" Behind him, two other shooters were playing Fort-Nite on the Big Screen, and there was another one making a ham and cheese sandwich in the kitchen. He'd just slid his knife into the jar of mayonnaise.

Kammron kept his head down. "Say B, I got forty dollars man. I need some of that Magic box. Do me good, baby boy. Let me get five for the forty?" He continued to hug himself.

The Shooter snapped. "Nigga, you gon' get dollar for dollar in the work you pay for. We don't give out no plays. You got forty dollars you get foe vials it's as simple as that. Where is your money?"

"Aahhh man." Kammron slid his hand into his pocket and came up with a .380. He turned with lightning speed and pressed the barrel to the shooter's high-yellow forehead and pulled the trigger.

Boom!

The shooter saw the flash, then felt the fire burn his skin. The bullet traveled through the meat of his forehead and knocked a chunk out of his skull, before it lodged into his brain, and stopped him from thinking. His head jerked backward, then Kammron was kicking him in the chest as hard as he could. Duke rushed into the house with his Gauge barking.

Boom!

His first bullet took half of the head off the man that was in the kitchen making the sandwich. He twisted around and fell face-first to the kitchen floor jerking in a puddle of blood. His second bullet blew a hole into one of the Fort-Nite players. The man fell backward over the couch and died immediately. The other Fort-Nite player started bucking at him and Kammron back to back by use of a Glock 9. Kammron fell to his knees and let his .380 ride.

Bock! Bock! Bock! Bock!

His bullets crashed into the television screen and caused it to explode. It fell from the wall with fire and smoke billowing out of it. Duke dropped the Gauge because it was empty of bullets. He pulled a .40 Cal from his waist, and dove to the floor, low crawling across it.

"Get up, fuck nigga. Ain't no way you finna escape these slugs!" he hollered.

The shooter remained behind the couch. "Fuck you niggas want man? I ain't did shit to y'all. If y'all want the Magic, it's a brick of it in the backroom. Take that shit and go!"

Kammron slowly made his way around the couch. He was out for blood. When he got to the edge of it, he peeked around it and saw a hint of the shooters' thigh. He aimed and bucked at it.

Bocka! Bocka! Bocka!
His bullets zipped from his gun and one of them grazed the shooter's thigh. The man hollered out in pain and started firing in every direction panicking. He could feel the stinging from his injury. "What the fuck y'all want? You ain't gotta kill me, please man."

Duke knew they were on the clock. They'd been firing their weapons for over three minutes which meant by this time somebody had to have called the law, and they had to be en route. He knew they had to crush this last shooter and get on with their day. They couldn't risk leaving him behind. He'd already seen Kammron's face. He signaled to Kammron to keep him talking.

Kammron nodded. "Say, man, we wanna know what you Yonkers niggas are on? Why the fuck y'all targeting, Kammron, and his crew? After he let y'all come over and eat in Harlem."

The shooter squeezed his wound. A trace of blood oozed over his fingers. "That shit is up to, Jason. He merged with them Vega boys, and they put the chips up on Kammron and Jimmy's head. That's two million dollars. You know damn well won't nobody gon' duck that money."

Duke continued to low crawl, he waved at Kammron. When he came to the other end of the couch, he signaled for Kammron to jump up, and buss. Kammron understood the signal and did exactly that. He jumped up and fired a shot over the couch. As soon as he did the shooter fell to his back and bussed twice. His bullets shot through the ceiling before his gun clicked empty.

Duke jumped up and rushed to stand over him. "This is Harlem, Son."

Boom! Boom! Boom! Boom!

Then he and Kammron was running from the apartment, and out of the building.

****

Later that night, Kammron sat on the floor of his bedroom with a belt tied around his arm. He eased the needle into his arm and pushed down on the feeder until the dope entered his system. His eyes rolled into the back of his head. He smacked his dry lips and moaned out loud.

"Happy Birthday, Mama, I'm missing you like crazy Queen. This shit got me all fucked up." He pulled the needle out of his left arm and set it on the lamp table.

Duke came out of the hallway and flopped on his bed. "Yo', you ready to go and holla at, Jimmy. This nigga been hitting my line up like crazy. He say it's imperative we don't miss this meeting."

Kammron waved Duke off and closed his eyes. "Fuck, Jimmy man. The God ain't got shit to say to him. Far as I'm concerned, I done already said what I needed too. If he ain't took heed, I don't know what the fuck to tell him. Besides, I got a nice high going. This new shit from Kaleb is off the ringer. Got me feeling breezy as a bitch."

Duke looked him over and stood up. The room smelled as if Kammron needed a shower. This was usually how things went when you started using that raw though. Most addicts didn't like to wash their asses because they felt the heroin kept them higher as long as their pores remained closed. Duke swore he would never let himself get like that. He didn't give a fuck how good a drug was he wasn't going to allow it to dictate how he washed and cared for himself.

"Yeah, well, I'm finna go and see what's really good. One of the smartest ways for a man to know what his enemy is up to is to hear him out. I might be walking into a blindside, and then again, I might not be. Either way, I gotta know what, Jimmy got on his mind, especially knowing that the Vega's put a million dollars on his head. Gotta have every nigga in New York trying to take a shot at him now that the word has been out for a few days."

Kammron nodded out, his chin was resting on his chest. Drool leaked out of the side of his mouth. He was like this for a full minute but coherent. He opened his eyes. "I don't give a fuck what you do. Make sure you tell, Jimmy, I said to kiss my ass, and that I will never turn Harlem back over to him. Tell that greedy son of a bitch, I'm willing to die for this borough." Kammron's eyes got heavy again, then he was nodding out. The music played loudly inside of his head. He smiled and turned it into a quick frown while he dozed.

Duke mugged him for a long time. He shook his head and opened a window in the room so some fresh air could come inside of it. "As soon as the meeting is over, I'ma let you know what's good. Be smooth nigga, I got Hittas all around on high alert. Love." He stepped into the hallway and closed the door.

While walking down the hallway he looked to his left and saw one of the guest bedroom doors open. In that room, on the bed, were two duffle bags filled with cash. There was so much money stuffed inside the bags they were over spilled with cash all over the bed. Duke stopped and stood in front of the door for a full minute, before closing it shut.

T.J. Edwards

Chapter 16

"Duke the muthafuckin' God! What it do, Kid. I'm surprised you even had enough gall to show up here. That's more than I can say for, Kammron," Jimmy quipped and laughed. He held his arms out like a cross and allowed Duke to walk into the warehouse with his two bodyguards behind him, both men were heavily armed.

Duke extended his hand and shook Jimmy's. "First thing first, keep my man's name out of your mouth especially if you finna be kicking that dumb shit. This one hunnit percent loyalty, right here." Jimmy rubbed his chin and looked Duke over.

Jimmy had ten armed Jamaicans behind him, eight of the ten held machetes in their hands. They were looking for any reason to murder Duke. Jimmy had instilled a deep hatred inside of his Shottas for Kammron, and anybody that was loyal to him.

"Duke, I hope the last thing you think you finna do is come here and tell me what to do? I don't know what that nigga, Kammron, let you do out there in Harlem, right now. But you ain't finna do none of that shit here. I'm letting you know that, right now.

Duke scoffed. "I see we starting this shit off on the wrong foot. Look I ain't come here to argue with you, Jimmy. I came here because I respect you, and thought it was in my best interest if I came as an ambassador to Harlem in the name of, Killa Kamm."

"Ambassador?" Jimmy took a seat at the head of the table. Two of his Jamaican Shottas came and stood directly behind him protectively inside of the banquet hall. Jimmy had all the blinds closed, and they sat under the illumination of a red light. Jimmy had his hair down around the sides of his face.

139

He looked like a pimp or something. He glared at Duke. "Kid, you ain't no muthafuckin' Ambassador to my borough. And, Kammron, ain't running shit. The only reason I let that, nigga stay where he is for so long is because I been getting shit right in, Jamaica. We need as many hands on deck as possible. That's the only way Harlem can be taken to the next level. That nigga, Kammron ain't doing shit but playin' wit' his life, and I mean that on everything I love."

Duke sucked his teeth and felt his anger rising. He looked over at the Jamaicans, then back to Jimmy! "Jimmy, why you called this sit-down? What's on your brain?"

"I wanted to holla at, Kammron face to face so we can get an understanding before I release my troops." When he said this another five Jamaicans came from the side room of the banquet hall with machetes in their hands and stood behind Jimmy.

Their faces were painted all green and their dreads were long and bushy looking. Jimmy leaned forward on the table and looked into Duke's eyes. "You see ain't no muthafucka playing games. Kammron, the only one. For as long as I've known you, Duke, you've always been one of those super, street, smart type niggas. So, you should know y'all ain't finna survive without me sitting at the head. The streets barking, Son. They say Kammron got a habit like the average dope addict in Harlem. Now tell me something. How the fuck is a dope addict gone be a King Pin? How is he gon' help you chase millions, think about it?"

Duke thought about the state Kammron was in the last time he saw him. He looked bad and smelled even worse. He didn't know how much longer, Kammron could possibly function before the drugs took him all the way under. That worried him, but he knew better than to show any weaknesses in front of Jimmy.

Duke sat back in his seat. "Nigga, I don't give a fuck what the streets barking about. The God is straight, I been making money hand over fist ever since I been back from Philly, and it's all been because of, Kammron. He true Harlem, that's more than I can say for yo' ass. Seem like you wanna be one of them dread heads if you ask me?"

The Jamaicans grumbled and grew impatient. They wanted Jimmy to give the order so they could make an example out of Duke.

Jimmy frowned and his eyes became blank. "Duke, tell that nigga, Kammron to step down and come underneath me. Or I can't be responsible for what's about to happen to all you, niggas. This is my last and final warning," when he said this Duke saw twenty more Jamaicans appear on the upstairs balcony.

They also had machetes in their hands. Duke could tell a few of them were female because they had breasts and curvy bodies.

Duke sighed in defeat. "Nigga you already know that fool, Kammron, don't listen to nobody. Besides, you shouldn't be trying to go to war with him when you got this fuck nigga by the name of Showbiz putting a million dollars on your head? Why the fuck you ain't went at them Vega boys? What you think the family over in Harlem is an easier target a something?"

"A million dollars—fuck is you talking about? "Jimmy sat up and lowered his eyes into slits.

Duke smiled. "Aahhh, Kid, you didn't know? Yeah, you musta been fuckin' around in Jamaica too long. Well, let me make shit perfectly clear. Them Vega boys put a million dollars on yo' head, and a million dollars on, Kammron's head. Ironically because he was sticking up for you when they tried to pay him to infiltrate your circle and ice yo ass. It don't matter how much y'all do or don't get along, Kid, ain't finna let no mafucka shit on you like that," Duke lied. He knew they weren't equipped to fight two wars at once. They already had their plates full with the Yonkers niggas. They couldn't add on Jimmy's Jamaicans as well. He needed to get Jimmy on board to help them go at the Vega boys, and quite possibly the Yonkers crew as well. Then he and Kammron could always do Jimmy in when it was all said and done.

Jimmy stood up. "That bitch nigga, Showbiz. He still gunning for me. And you mean to tell me it's a million dollars on my life?"

"Cash, that family ain't playin' wit' you. They got every mafucka in Harlem trying to become a millionaire at your expense. The only mafuckas been holding you down is, Kammron and Duke Da God.".

Jimmy lowered his head and looked down at the table. He was so sick of the Vega family. Sick of their dirty underhanded politics and antics. He felt it was time to clap back at them. If there was a million dollars on his head, then there was no telling who would take the contract. He imagined there would be a bunch of people, even groups. New York was full of cutthroats and crooks. He would be forced to watch his back everywhere he looked even more than usual.

"That ain't it, he gave the contract to these niggas from Yonkers. A kat named, Jason specifically. They in New York, right now looking for an opportunity to lace you and Kammron. When you hit up my phone for the first time yesterday me and Kammron was getting ready to mount up so we could go at these clowns, before we take that trip to Havana to body Showbiz, and his punk ass brother Tristan. So, instead of going to handle our bidness, Kammron sent me to holla at you, while he keeps our troops ready for war. Then when I get here, you're talking all of this bullshit. It's insane!"

Jimmy kept his head down and took a deep breath then exhaled slowly. He raised his head and looked around at his Shottas again. "You, betta not be lying to me, Duke. Right now, you really ain't on my list for annihilation. But if I find out you're lying you've moved to the top of the list. You and your family, I ain't finna play with none of you muthafuckas. You hear what I'm saying, right now?"

Duke wanted to spit in his face and blow his brains all over the oak wooden table. "Yeah, I hear you Jimmy, but I ain't got no reason to lie to you. All you gotta do is holla at any one of your sources in north New York. Shid, maybe all of New York period. Word is spreading all over the city. I'm sure it's on Facebook by now. But no matter how you confirm what I'm telling you, just know everything I am saying is authentic. Take heed or be blindsided."

"And you said this nigga from Yonkers name is, Jason?" Jimmy asked.

Duke nodded. "Yep, it's him and a whole bunch of so-called killas sniffing around the Apple looking for you and Kammron. In fact, we finna spend the next week or so hunting them mafuckas until we fully wipe them out. Then we're coming for the Vegas, but it seems like ain't nobody strong enough to go at them," Duke said hoping it would bruise Jimmy's ego.

Jimmy smacked his lips. "You got the game fucked up. Them Vega niggas can suck my dick. Ain't nobody worried about them. In fact, I'ma send my Shottas to get at them and to fuck over these Yonkers niggas. Mafuckas ain't prepared for the level of attack I can bring down on a nigga's ass." He slammed his hand on the table. "But got dammit what I said before about Kammron stepping down I really mean it. If by the time this war is over, he ain't stepped to the side we're going to have a serious misunderstanding. Tell him I said, right now, we're comrades in war, but as soon as this shit is over there can only be one king of Harlem. You're dismissed."

Duke walked out of Jimmy's establishment with a sly smile across his face. Now all he had to do was get Kammron on board. They could allow Jimmy to do all the heavy lifting. They'd clean up what he left behind before they knocked him off as well. Duke had some things going on inside of his brain that nobody else knew about. Things that were guaranteed to be a complete game-changer for the make-up of Harlem in its entirety.

****

Shana paced back and forth inside of the living room with her hands on her hips. She'd been crying for an hour straight. She was steaming mad at what Kammron had done. She was tired of being under his thumb. Tired of fearing what he would do next. She clutched her cellphone tighter in her hand and tried to gather up the nerve to do what she needed to do. She took a deep breath and dialed the number to the homicide detective. She allowed the phone to ring three times before it was answered.

"Hello, this is detective Ross speaking. May I ask who's calling?"

Shana cleared her throat. "Um yes, my name is Shana Rodriquez. I would like to report a murder."

Detective Ross sat upright in his chair. The six-foot, Jewish man adjusted his cellphone in his hand and spoke softly. "Yes, Ms. Rodriguez, go ahead I'm listening."

Duke came through the front door and closed it behind him. Shana hung up her phone and turned around to face him. She still had tears sailing down her cheeks. Duke saw this and immediately became vexed. He looked around her small apartment and saw it was empty. There wasn't a lick of furniture anywhere in sight. He pulled her to him and brushed her long hair with his hand. "Baby, what the hell happened? Were you robbed or something?"

Shana began to really break down. "No, Kammron came, and he had five dudes with him. They took all the furniture and all of my jewelry. He said that if he bought shit, so it belonged to him, and I was cut off. He said if I want all the nice things that I had, you would have to buy them for me. The only things he left was Junior's clothes and toys. He's so petty for this shit," she growled in anger. She hugged Duke tighter and buried her face in his chest.

Duke palmed the back of her head and started to shake. He was heated. It seemed Kammron was trying to go above and beyond to make Shana miserable, and so far, he was doing a good job at it.

Duke kissed Shana on the top of the head and held her protectively. "Ma, don't even worry, I got you. In fact, what I want you to do, right now is to get on your phone and go on a furniture sight of your choice and furnish the whole house. When you have everything in your cart let me know, I'll pull the trigger on it for you. Everything you had I'ma upgrade you, I promise. Now how does that sound?"

This only made Shana cry harder. "Why do you care about me so much, Duke? How long are you going, too? When are you going to dog me out like he did? Please tell me because I wanna know," she cried.

Duke held her and lowered his face to the top of her head. He didn't like seeing any female cry, but especially not his daughter, or Shana. He didn't understand how it happened so quickly, but he actually loved and cared about her. He didn't agree with how Kammron was treating her, and it was taking everything inside of him to not go over to Kammron's crib and get in his ass.

"I ain't going nowhere, Shana. I got you, Boo. I'm ten toes down for you, and I ain't looking to leave your side. You're a Queen Goddess, and I'm yo muthafuckin' King. We're in this shit together for the long haul. I'm not gon' leave you out here on yo' own. Trust and believe the God got more respect for you, and for our struggle than that."

Shana wanted to believe the words coming out of his mouth, but she had always heard the saying: *birds of a feather flock together*. Kammron was a dirty Harlem nigga, and as far as she knew Bonkers had been the same way. She couldn't see Duke being any different. But she hoped and prayed he was.

"Duke, I don't understand why you care about me the way you do? But I am thankful for you. I promise to do all I can for you. I wanna prove to you that all Harlem women aren't as Ratchet as everybody makes us out to be. I'ma be ten toes down for you as well." She wrapped her arms around him and felt her cellphone buzzing in her back pocket.

She knew it could only be the detective calling her back. She didn't know when she would return his call, all she knew was that it would be soon.

Duke turned her around facing him. He held her small face with his big hands. "Listen to me, Shana, Kammron is my nigga, but I don't want you asking him for shit else. I got you from here on out. Anything you need or want, hit me up and I'll make sure you got it as soon as I can. You understand? That means from here on out you are my responsibility until you are strong enough to get out there and stand on your own two feet, I got you. Can you promise me this?"

Shana's eyes were tearing up again. She hated herself for being so emotional, but she couldn't help it. Duke was the nicest man she'd ever met, and she only prayed he remained that way. "I promise, Duke, and once again thank you so much. I really mean that." She stepped on to her tippy toes and kissed his lips.

Duke cuffed her rounded ass and tongued her down. She tasted sweet and forbidden. Her vulnerability only made him want to protect her even more. Protect her from the cold world that was seemingly run by Kammron, and niggas like Jimmy. He also wanted to protect her fragile heart.

He kissed her forehead. "I got you, Boo. Word to, Jehovah, I got you."

T.J. Edwards

Chapter 17

Kammron walked around his new Bentley truck that he'd just pulled out of the detailing garage. It was purple and yellow, sitting on forty-inch Parelli's. He pulled his quart length mink snug over him, and a broad smile spread across his face. Snow was falling from the sky, even though the sun shined. Kammron placed his arm around one of the light-skinned sale's girls he'd been peeping inside the shop. She had come out to make sure that everything was good and to his liking.

"Shorty you see this shit. This mafucka righteous. It's painted butter and jelly and sitting on forty-inch Parelli's." This mafucka is something you cop when you know you're a boss. You wanna come and fuck with the Set?" He asked her walking around his truck. He eyed it real close and couldn't help smiling. He had come a long way. "What's your name anyway?"

"Henny," she said with a voice so soft it made Kammron feel some type of way. "What's the Set? I thought you were that major dude from Harlem everybody has been talking about?"

"That is me, baby girl. I'm the one and only, Killa Kamm, King of the Set. Right now, I'm in need of a young Queen that look as bad as yo' lil' ass. So, what you say? You wanna come fuck wit' me and leave this nine to five as job alone?"

Henny looked toward the open door of the shop. It had been her first job. Maris the store owner had hired her because she went to church with her mother. She was set to be eighteen in a few months, and the lady had decided to take a chance on her. She didn't know how she would look if she just up and left her job and rolled off with some kingpin.

"I don't know, Kamm, I think my mother would be pretty mad at me. Right now, we're struggling with the bills at home, and she's kind of depending on the paycheck that I bring home every few weeks." The wind blew, this made her pop her collar so she could protect her ears.

"How much money you make working here, Goddess?" Kammron was looking for an opening to jack on her. He knew she couldn't be making much more than minimum wage. He stared into her light brown eyes and watched her long curly hair blow in the wind. She looked so sexy, like jailbait.

"I make four hundred every two weeks guaranteed, and if I can convince some of the customers to purchase some of the items or accessories for their cars and trucks, I also get a five percent commission off each sale. So, it's not bad."

Kammron dug into his Marc Jacob leather jacket and pulled a ridiculous knot from his pocket. He peeled off a few hunnits. "Fuck this job you rolling with the Kid now. You just got bumped into the Goddess open seat of Harlem."

Henny took the money and thumbed through it. When she was sure all she saw was hundred dollar bills she became dizzy. "Kamm, are you sure, you're going to give me all of this?"

Kammron nodded. "Go in there and get your purse. You finna roll off the lot with me, right now. Hurry up!"

Henny nodded her head and hurried inside. Kammron watched the way her ass jiggled as she made haste into the store. He couldn't wait to get her lil' ass back to his suite. He had plans for her. Henny ran into the store and grabbed her purse. She took one look at Maris and put her head down.

"Henny, baby, what's the matter? Where are you going?" Maris asked her.

"I'm sorry, Mrs. Maris, but I quit," Henny said with her head still down.

"*You quit!* Baby, what are you talking about?"

"I can't explain, right now Mrs. Maris. I gotta talk to you later." She ran out into the parking lot over to Kammron's truck.

Kammron held the door open and sat back like a boss. Her perfume invaded his nostrils louder with the door closed. "Shorty you don't even know it but I'm about to change your life."

Henny allowed the automatic seatbelt to click around her. She batted her naturally long eyelashes and couldn't deny how nervous she felt. "I don't know what you mean by that but here goes nothing." She laughed.

"Say shorty, you ever been in a private jet before?"

Henny shook her head. "No, I've never been on a plane before either."

Kammron nodded. "A true lil' hood bitch then, that's just what I was looking for. We finna change all of that tonight."

Kammron had business to take care of with Ponchie and he was sending a Chopper to pick him up. The chopper would carry Kammron from New York to Washington D.C. and back. Kammron figured it would be a perfect time to flex on Henny. He still couldn't believe how bad she was.

****

Three hours later, Kammron laid Henny in the middle of the king-size bed and opened her thick thighs as far as she would allow him too. He sucked two fingers into his mouth, and rubbed them from side to side, playing with her bald pussy.

"Say, baby girl you mean to tell me you shave your pussy every single day?" He opened the lips, placed his nose right on her little hole and sniffed hard.

Henny felt weird, it was the first time any man had been between her thighs. She prayed she didn't smell weird to him and wondered why he kept sniffing her down there. "I don't grow hair there yet. My mother was the same way," she responded and started to shake.

Kammron held open her golden lips far enough to make out her glistening pink. He took his tongue and swiped up and down her groove, swallowing her juices that had come out of her.

He closed his eyes and smiled. "Aahhh, hell yeah this some fresh pussy, right here. How many niggas you been with, Henny?"

"What? *Nobody*, I've never been with anybody before. My mother don't let me do nothing like that. She keeps me in the house."

Kammron sucked her clitoris into his mouth, sucked hard on it. His tongue shot back and forth across it. Her nub seemed to get larger and larger. Henny arched her back, began to shake like crazy. The feeling kept getting better and better. Her nipples were rock hard on her chest. They were so spiked that they hurt. The fact that they were in a private jet only added to her state of arousal.

The feeling was overwhelming. "Uhhhh, Kammron!"

Kammron was already on bidness. He began to make savage love to Henny's young pussy. Slurping, and smacking over her juices. He took two digits and slid them as far as they could go inside of her womb. When he got to the barrier inside, he started to cheese. "Aahhh, hell yeah, you telling the truth."

Henny felt a slight discomfort with his fingers invading her gap. She wanted to clamp her thighs closed but decided against it. She didn't know what that would make Kammron do, and she was too afraid to roll the dice. She felt him peel her sex lips all the way apart, then he was driving her insane.

She gripped her C cup titties and squeezed them together. "Unnhh-unnhhh, in, oh my—"

Kammron's tongue flicked at her nub faster and faster, then he was sucking on it.

Henny screamed and humped into his mouth. Her coochie was leaking worse than ever. It felt as if Kammron was performing a magic trick on her box. "Yes, Kammron, yes! Yes, I don't—know—unn—what—you're doing, but—uunnhhh!" She sat all the way up, and came hard, screaming. Then she threw herself back on the bed, pinching her nipples, and pulling them through her blouse.

Kammron sucked and licked in between the crux of her thighs. He ran his tongue inside her belly button, and all the way up until he was forced to remove her bra, and blouse from her body, exposing her dark brown nipples that looked like pacifiers. They stood up heavily engorged. The sight of them drove Kammron crazy. He straddled her body and leaned down. His neck was covered with a million dollars' worth of jewelry. They rubbed against her forehead until he scooted down and began sucking on ripe nipples one at a time while rubbing her naked pussy.

"You got a thick ass, you know that?"

Henny moaned and opened her thick thighs wider. "Yes, I know, that's what they say at my school."

Kammron snickered and pulled his dick out of his Polo boxers. He ran the head up and down her slimy groove. Then dipped the head slightly into her opening, until she dug her nails into his back. "Ssss—wait!" She winced.

Kammron continued to play with her pussy. "It's okay baby, I ain't gon' hurt you. This is part of the process if you finna sit on the throne of Harlem beside me. Ain't you ready to ball hard beside the God for the rest of your life?" He asked running his thumb around her clit over and over again.

Henny jerked again and again. Whatever Kammron was doing to her felt amazing. She didn't know if she was really ready to take all of him, but she was damn sure ready to try. "Okay, try again, I'm ready."

Kammron stroked his piece, he smashed the head into her meaty lips, and slowly eased his way into her. When he felt the barrier inside of her box, he leaned down and sucked on her neck. "A'ight ma, now this part gon' make you feel some type of way, but bare wit' me." He rocked back and forth real gently, then cocked back and slammed forward as hard as he could.

Henny yelled and bit into his shoulder blade. Her nails dug into his back. Tears crept down her face, she felt him fucking her at full speed now. She went from feeling a bunch of pain to a mixture of pleasure and pain. The feeling got better and better until she was moaning and encouraging him to fuck her harder without actually saying it.

"Oh! Oh! Oh, Kammron—shoot!"

Kammron popped his back and dug deeper and deeper. Her pussy was so tight he felt suffocated. In his mind, there was nothing like new pussy. New fresh pussy that felt snug and hot as a sauna. He sucked harder on her neck and kept right on fucking as hard as he could. They bounced up and down on the bed while the private jet flew over New York City on its way to Washington D.C.

****

Forty minutes into the flight Kammron pulled out of Henny and rolled on his back breathing heavy. He'd cum inside her pussy five times and his piece was still hard. Henny had that snapper. Kammron knew he was going to love jumping up and down inside of her. He pulled her body on top of his and cuffed her ass. "You okay, baby?"

Henny felt like her kitty was on fire. She was tired and extremely depleted. All she wanted to do was to sleep. She nodded. "Yeah, I'm good, just exhausted." She closed her eyes and snuggled up to him.

Kammron laughed. "That's what good fuckin' do to you. But I need you to sit up because we got one more order of bidness, baby girl if you finna roll wit' me."

Henny's eyes were so heavy, she wanted to fall asleep on him. He smacked her ass cheeks, only then did she scoot up and lay her head on his chest. "What now, Kammron?"

Kammron frowned. "First off, you gon' call me, Daddy. My name ain't Kammron when it comes to you, you got that?"

She nodded. "Okay."

"Next thing is this—" Kammron reached over and pulled the tray of China White from under the bed. It was already separated into four lines. He held the tray on their laps and handed her a straw. "Huh, this what I want you to do." He took two of the lines and coughed. Wiped his nose and laid his straw to the side of the tray. "Do it just like that."

Henny's eyes got big. "Are you serious? My mother always told me to stay away from stuff like that. I'm sorry but it doesn't seem like a good idea. No thank you." She placed the straw back on the tray and snuggled up to Kammron.

Kammron allowed her to hold him for a short while, and then he wiggled out of her grasp. "Aahhh, you ain't fuckin' wit' it?"

She closed her eyes and yawned, then covered her mouth. "No, but thank you anyway."

Kammron grunted and sat all the way up. "Then get dressed. You finna get the fuck off my Chopper, right now."

Henny laughed. "Stop playin', Kammron. Now let's get some sleep, I'm begging you," she whined.

Kammron sat the platter back on the floor inside of the huge Helicopter. "I'm serious, Ma, get dressed? I'm finna slap a parachute on yo ass and you finna get the fuck out of my sights, right now. I can't even look at you." He climbed out of the bed and remained hunched over because of the low ceiling. He was ready to flip the fold-out bed back into the sofa that was welded to the floor.

Henny saw he was dead serious and got sick on her stomach. When she looked out of the Helicopter's window, she saw that they were flying over a large body of water. It freaked her out. "Kammron are you really about to make me jump if I don't do what you want me to do off the platter?"

"You muthafuckin' right? It's a billion lil' young bitches out there that a love to be in your shoes. You know what I'm finna do. I'm finna go and find me one of those hoes." He pulled a parachute from the emergency chest and tossed it on the bed.

Now Henny was completely freaking out. She climbed from the bed and pulled the platter from under it. She picked up a straw and placed it inside of her nose. With a string inhale she cleared a line and fell back coughing. Her eyes watered.

Kammron smirked and proceeded to calm down. "Let me show you how you gotta do this, baby girl. Daddy don't want you to hurt yo' lil' lungs." Before the helicopter landed, Henny was hooked, and right where Kammron needed her to be.

Chapter 18

The next week Ponchie flooded Kammron with two hundred bricks of pure Coke. As soon as they hit the streets of Harlem they seemed to disappear. Kammron had his workers go into overdrive. Each worker that was in charge of the white worked sixteen-hour shifts or more and wasn't allowed to clock out until their quota was fulfilled for the day. Kammron ran a tight ship with Duke as his overseer. Both men ran the game with an iron fist.

By the beginning of the next week, Kammron was flying back out to D.C. where Ponchie sent him back on his personal chopper with four hundred bricks of Yay. This time it took Kammron and his crew two weeks to get rid of it, which he considered light work. At the same time, they were moving the Ponchie bricks they were flying through key after key of the work that Kaleb was hitting them with. The money was coming in by the bundles so Kammron had Kamina creating offshore accounts, along with investing in the stock market, and real estate.

He made sure Kammron's dirty money was funneled into the local businesses and washed clean before he sent it across seas where it would wind up in an offshore account. Kamina knew the only way a player could last a long time in the game was if they made sure Uncle Sam got his due. So, it was imperative to him that Kammron and the Set gave Uncle Sam his due.

Duke was another story, Kamina helped him reopen two community centers, and a boys and girls club inside of Harlem that had previously been shut down for one reason or the other. Duke wound up coming off four hundred thousand dollars just to get those doors reopened, but for him, it was the best money ever spent. He knew there was a war brewing, and the streets of Harlem were about to turn bloody. He wanted to make sure the Youth had somewhere to go. Somewhere they could play after school. His community centers, and Boys and Girls club was also a place Shana could sit on staff as a counselor, and liaison. The pay for her wouldn't start off the greatest, but it was a place that would give her a sense of purpose.

In the third week after Duke's places of refuge had been opened, Jason pulled up on him and Shana as they were coming out of the Boys and Girls club preparing to get into his Benz. Jason rolled down the mirror tinted windows to his black on black BMW and one of his Hittas pointed an AK-47 out the window.

Jason laughed. "Say bitch niggas hop in, let a mafucka holla at you for a minute," though he said it as a request, he meant it as an order.

Duke stood in front of Shana, shielding her from the shooter. "Yeah, a'ight nigga that's cool, just let my Shorty roll off."

Jason shrugged his shoulders. "I don't give a fuck what that bitch do. She ain't got shit to do with this. A mafucka need to holla at you. So, get ya ass in the car. I ain't gon' ask again." The back door swung open and one of the masked niggas from Yonkers motioned for Duke to get inside the car.

Duke held up one finger. He turned around and kissed a shaking Shana on the lips. "Look, Shorty, it's good. Let me fuck wit' Kid nem for a minute. I'll check you out at the crib."

Shana held onto him. "Baby, please don't go with them. I can tell they're up to no good. Don't do this, please I'm begging you," she cried placing her face into his armpit.

She had the worst luck, she just knew as soon as things started going good, God was going to take him away from her. "Baby, fuck it, just let me go with you. Whatever they finna do to you they can do it to me, too."

"Sound like a plan to me," Jason said, as three of his Hittas hopped out of the car with their assault rifles brandished.

A black van pulled to the back of Jason's whip and Duke and Shana were tossed inside of it.

****

Jimmy loosened the cap on the gallon of gasoline and poured it on the sleeping pair inside the bedroom. Tristan was the first to open his eyes as he felt the liquid splash all over his face. He felt like he was being drowned. His eyes opened and pinned onto Jimmy's angry face.

"Jimmy, what the fuck? How did you get in here?"

Jimmy grabbed him by the throat as one of the Jamaicans lit a match behind them. He placed his forehead against Tristan's. "You bitch ass, nigga. You always making it seem like we're on the same page, then I find out we're not."

Tristan's fiancée opened her eyes before she could scream one of the masked Jamaicans placed his hand over her mouth and a machete to her neck. "Shut ya trap you peasant. Don't you dare let out another sound."

Jimmy glared at Tristan. "Explain yourself?"

Tristan swallowed his spit. The scent of gasoline was heavy in the air. "Every time you and I come to an understanding I always hold up my end. But I can't speak for my brother. He does what he wants."

Jimmy slid a Machete from his inside sheath and held the blade to his neck. "I gave you the benefit of the doubt because word through the underworld was that Showbiz was going to be passed up for the throne. And it was going to be handed to you, but now I'm hearing that Showbiz may be taking that seat when your father steps down. If that's the case, then what the fuck do I need you for?" He slowly slid the blade across Tristan's neck until a trickle of blood appeared.

Tristan's fiancée screamed into the Jamaican's hand as soon as she saw the blood. She wondered how the bandits had gotten into the Vega mansion when it was so heavily guarded. Something wasn't right and she felt it.

Tristan tensed up. "My father Vito has already started preparing me to take over as his successor. Showbiz found out, he and I are no longer seeing eye to eye. In fact, he wants me dead."

Jimmy was seconds away from slashing Tristan's throat until he heard this last part. "Come again?"

"You heard what I said, Jimmy. My brother, Showbiz wants me dead, and my entire side of the Vega operation dismantled. He says our father is off his rocker, and unfit to make sound decisions regarding our family so therefore he is taking the throne on his own accord. It's probably the reason you were able to so easily break into this mansion tonight."

Jimmy released the Machete from his neck and thought about it. They only had to overpower three guards who didn't put up much of a fight. Jimmy knew how the Vegas got down. They were extremely powerful in Havana it was next to impossible trying to penetrate them. So, the fact that he was able to get to Tristan so easily couldn't have been a coincidence. At the same time, he wasn't willing to trust Tristan at his word. He snapped his finger. One of his Jamaican henchmen stepped forward and placed a wet cloth soaked in chloroform over Tristan's face, and knocked him out. He did the same to Tristan's screaming fiancée.

"I'm finna see just how true this really is." He gave the signal. "Wrap them up in the sheets, they're going on a trip."

****

Jason cocked back and swung as hard and fast as he could. His fist crashed into Duke's jaw and rocked him hard. The sound of skin on knuckle was loud inside the basement. Jason grabbed Duke once again by his shirt and prepared to swing for the tenth time. He already had Duke bleeding like a stuck pig. He cocked back, and punched him straight on, knocking out both of Duke's front teeth. He stepped back and shook his hand out.

Duke spit a glob of blood on the concrete and continued to breathe hard. One of his eyes had closed up. He looked over at Shana as she was chained to the wall beside him. She was untouched and as long as she was, he was willing to endure whatever came at him. He saw his two teeth on the floor in front of him and ran his tongue over his bloody gums where they had come out.

Jason stepped forward and took a hold of his chin. He held it roughly. "Nigga, I'ma ask you one more time, where is Kammron's safe house? And what are the combinations to his safes? You tell me that, and you can walk out of here. You and your, bitch."

Blood dripped from Duke's lip and chin. "I don't know where bruh keeps none of his shit. That—ain't—my bidness to know," Duke struggled to breathe. "Just take my safes—you can have that chump change—just—let my woman go," Duke huffed and puffed. He swallowed blood once again and felt sick on the stomach.

Jason shook his head. "N'all fuck that, that's how you know when a nigga ain't really fuckin' with nothing if he is so quick to give it up. Every nigga and they mama know, you ain't nothing but a flunkey. Kammron, don't give a fuck about you just like he don't give a fuck about Bonkers bitch ass. He left that fool in a coma and fucked his bitch more times than he did, and they grew up together as right-hand men. You don't hold nowhere near that kind of prestige. As soon as it befits him, he gon' chew you up and spit you out," Jason sneered at him. "Now tell me what the fuck I need to know? Where the fuck is this nigga's safe house? What's the codes to his safe? Where he lay his head?"

Duke held his silence, his whole body hurt. He knew for a fact one of his ribs were broken. The pain was too intense. He struggled to breathe and even when he did it came out labored, and wheezy.

"A'ight, I see how you wanna play this shit." He grabbed the chainsaw off the table and pulled the string. It took him a few times, but then the engine revved? He held the blade in front of Duke's face and revved it again. "This is your last chance to talk."

Duke was willing to die with his knowledge. While he believed some of the things were true about Kammron, and how he was perceived, it wasn't enough to make him betray him. "Yo, fuck you, Kid. I hope you know how to use that muthafucka because I ain't telling you shit. Bury me in Harlem God, word to Uptown."

Jason broke out laughing. "Aw nigga, this blade ain't for you just yet. You see I understand that you got the heart of a Lion when it comes to some kamikaze type shit. However, deep down you truly is a pussy nigga because you're stuck on this bitch, right here. So, this saw is for her and not you." Jason revved the engine and stepped beside Shana. He lowered it and cut into the flesh of her shoulder.

Shana screamed as she felt the chainsawing into her vulnerable flesh. It felt like a steak knife sawing away at her. The pain was so great she pissed on herself. Her knees buckled. Jason took a step back with the bloody blade dripping. "Check dis out Duke, I'm just getting started. Now if you love this woman, you'll tell me what I need to know."

Shana groaned against her binds. Tears ran down her pretty face. She lowered her head and squeezed her eyes as tight as she could. "This ain't right, Duke, none of this shit is." She struggled against her binds once again with no success of breaking them.

Duke felt like crap, but he couldn't let on that Jason was getting to him. He knew if he let any weaknesses be known in front of the Yonkers Killa, he would use it against him. "Shana shut up, baby. Don't say another word!"

Shana bit into her bottom lip to keep silent. She didn't know what else to do. She thought about her son and wondered if she would ever be able to see him again. She didn't feel it was fair she should have to risk her life for Kammron when she knew damn well he didn't care about anyone else other than himself. But she loved Duke and she didn't feel that he would fail her.

Jason revved the chainsaw again. He walked toward her with the blade. "Say, Duke, this is fucked up man! You already know how Kammron from Harlem gets down. That nigga would never go through all this for nobody. Yousa savage for putting your girl through this man, but I guess!" Jason brought the blade toward Shana's neck and got ready to behead her right in front of Duke.

Shana closed her eyes and waited for the expected. The only person she could see behind her eyes was Junior, her son. She also thought about fighting against her attacker but knew it would have been a mock attempt. She was chained to a wall by her wrists. There was no way of getting around it. As the blade grew closer, she could smell the gasoline. The sound became loud in her ears.

Jason was inches away from her neck when Duke called out to him. "Waaiittt!"

Jason smiled with his back turned to Duke. He slowly eased his finger off the trig that caused the engine to rev like crazy. He turned around to face Duke. Then walked until he was standing in front of him. "Nigga, you got something you wanna say to me?"

Chapter 19

"How much is it going to take? What is it going to cost us for you to let my woman go, and for you to leave us the fuck alone?" While these were the words coming out of Duke's mouth, he wasn't thinking about anything other than revenge. He simply wanted to get them out of the sticky situation. He would deal with Jason and his Yonkers crew accordingly after that.

Jason rubbed his chin with one hand and held the chain saw in his other. "Word on the street is that Kammron got some serious M's put up. At least ten, nigga we ain't leaving Harlem, angling back to Yonkers until we got at least five of them, Jokers. That's the price for your shorty, right here, and time is running out. It looks like she's a bleeder." He nodded at Shana with his head.

Shana had blood oozing out of her wound as sweat saturated her face. She breathed heavy and hung tirelessly against her chains.

Duke swallowed and exhaled loudly. "Yo', if I can get you five million, you and yo' niggas a leave Harlem for good?"

Jason nodded. "You muthafuckin', right. But I'ma need that shit in cash, in less than twenty-four hours. If you ain't back here with that scratch by then, not only is this bitch finna get the bidness, but some of the homies made a pit stop to Philly, and we just so happened to stumble up on this lil' broad, too." He snapped his fingers and stood back with a mug on his face.

Duke's heart nearly fell out of his chest when he saw the way one of Jason's monsters were handling his daughter Deanna. The man held her by the back of her neck roughly. Her mouth was taped with silver duct tape, and she was crying. She had handcuffs on her wrists, and shackles on her six-year-old ankles.

Duke tried his best to break away from the chains. "Arrgh, dis ain't got nothin' to do with her. Let my muthafuckin' shorty go!"

Jason kneeled in front of the crying Deanna. He rubbed her face. "Aw po' baby, you're so pretty. You don't look nothing like yo' ugly ass daddy, luckily for you." He looked over at Duke and cheesed. "How old are you, baby girl?" He knew she couldn't answer him because her mouth was covered with the tape, but to be an asshole he placed his ear right on her duct tape. "I'm sorry, Sweetie, I can't hear you. You're going to have to speak up."

Deanna could only cry, she couldn't understand what was going on, and why the men had hurt her mommy, and took her away. Nothing made sense, if this was a game her father was playing, she didn't like it. It was too scary.

Jason stood up, grabbed a handful of Deanna's hair, and mugged Duke. "You got twenty-two hours to come up with my gwop. Find my cash or find both of these hoes floating in the Harlem River. Now that's word to, Uptown." He broke into laughter and gave the signal to his men so they could snatch up Duke and drop him off in a random place in New York.

****

Henny crawled nakedly cross the bed and climbed atop Kammron. She laid her cheek against his and rubbed the side of his face. "Daddy, I'm so turnt up I can't think straight. My whole body is tingling," she mumbled.

Kammron was high as a kite as well. They had spent the entire day shooting China. He felt like he was on a planet of euphoria. He licked his lips and rubbed his hands down the small of Henny's lower back until he was cuffing her ass. He still couldn't believe how strapped she really was. "Yo, it's like I told you, you fuck with me, you ain't her finna have to worry about nothing. It'll be smiles from here on out. That's what a daddy is supposed to do."

Henny dubbed her bald Kitty up and down Kammron's stomach, she left a trail of her essence. "Daddy, I'm so horny. I need you, I'm fiendin'." She slid her hand under her stomach and opened her sex lips, before slipping her middle finger up her box. The sensation coupled with the China was enough to make her shudder.

Kammron opened her ass cheeks and trailed a digit around her tight rosebud. He dipped his middle finger into her hole and pulled it back out. "I wanna fuck this young ass, Henny. Daddy wanna hit this back door. You wanna give me some of that?" He squeezed her ass again, his piece began to telescope against her body.

Henny felt it and moved up on his frame. She trapped the head of his piece between her sex lips, rotated her hips against his lap. Her eyes closed and rolled into the back of her head. "Mmm-mmm-mmm, Daddy! Unnhh-unnhhh-yes, Daddy!" Her coochie got wetter and wetter in a matter of seconds as she grinded against him. Kammron simply held her ass and laid back. What she was doing felt good. His fingers crept into her crevice, he played with her juices and sucked on her neck.

"Uhhhh, Daddy!" More jumping, and grinding. "Fuck me, please, please, Daddy. I'm begging you." Her kitty was on fire.

She grabbed a hold of Kammron's dick, and started to stuff him into her box, as soon as his head peeked through her entrance, she slammed down on him and started riding him as her breasts slapped up and down. "Unnhhh-unnhhh-unnhhh, Daddy! Daddy-ooo-ooo, fuck yes!" She held the top of the headboard for leverage and worked him.

Kammron leaned up and sucked one erect nipple, then the next. His tongue ran circles around each one. Then he was kissing in between the globes and licking up her sweat. Her pussy felt like a hot glove wrapped around his pipe. She was so wet it was running out of her and making a puddle under both of their asses.

"Yeah, baby, ride Daddy! Ride Daddy, ride Daddy—ride Daddy! Shit—ride me!" He gripped her cheeks and proceeded to slam her forward, making sure she was taking his entire length.

"Here I—uhhhh, here I—cum, Daddy! Fuck—uhhhh!" she screamed, and began working him as hard and as fast as she could. Then she was shaking, and her cat began to spit love juices all over him.

Kammron flipped her on her stomach and slightly parted her thighs. He smacked her ass and watched her chubby cheeks jiggle. He opened her booty wide and ran his tongue in circles around her rosebud. When he got it nice and dripping, he grabbed the K-Y from the dresser and stroked his piece with it, getting it nice and lubed. Then he slowly worked his dick into Henny's ass.

She grabbed ahold of the sheets and balled it into her small hand. "Unnhhh, Daddy." Her hand snuck between her thick thighs to manipulate her clit. She pinched and rolled her middle finger around it.

After Kammron pulled her up to all fours. He eased into her back door slowly and stroked her lovely at first, then speeded up the pace and proceeded to fuck her like a Porn star, digging deep into her backdoor.

Henny grinned and it didn't take long before she was loving what he was doing to her. As long as she kept her fingers on her clit, the China allowed all her sexual senses to be heightened times a hundred. "Fuck me, Daddy! Fuck me-fuck me, yes! Unnhhh, Daddy, yes-yes! I'm yours—I'm yours," she moaned.

Kammron watched his pipe run in and out of her. It drove him crazy. He slapped her ass hard, it jiggled and motivated him to go savage mode on her. "Uh-uh-uh-uh, uhhhh shit, Henny! Baby girl, Daddy—uhhhh!" He began cumming hard, slamming into her as deep as he could go. Then he was falling on top of her.

****

Duke felt like he couldn't breathe. He was running as fast as he could and had been ever since Jason's men dropped him off in Ruckers Park. When he made it onto Kammron's street he struggled to keep up the same pace. He made it to his stoop before he stopped to take a breather. His lungs felt as if they were inflamed. He swallowed his spit and could taste the blood mixed with mucus. He gathered himself and rushed up the steps beating on the door.

Kammron sat upright in bed. He grabbed a .40 Caliber from under his pillow, looked over and saw Henny sitting in the love seat just sliding the syringe into her vein. She pushed down on the feeder as her eyes rolled into the back of her head. Kammron jumped up and rushed into the hallway.

He ran to the front of the house naked and placed his back to the door. "Who the fuck is that beating on my door?"

Duke continued to try and catch his breath. "It's me, Kammron. Open the fuckin' door, B." Duke looked over his shoulder.

Three Expeditions pulled to the curb with Kammron's security inside of them. They were ready to annihilate Duke because at first, they couldn't identify him. But when they made him out, they pulled away from the curb and continued to make their rounds in the neighborhood.

"Duke why the fuck are you beating on the door like you're crazy? Have you lost your fuckin' mind?" Kammron snapped. He peeked out of the window and made sure it was actually him.

Duke held his head down. "Open the door, Kammron, I need your help. Please man, this sit is serious bidness."

Kammron took a step back and opened the door. He allowed Duke to step into the living room. Duke began to pace back and forth right away. Kammron locked the door back and turned around to face Duke. "What the fuck happened to your face, Duke?"

"Dem Yonkers niggas, B. Kid, they fucked me up, they got Shana and my daughter Deanna man." Duke felt like he was minutes away from becoming hysterical. He really didn't know what to do.

Kammron mugged him. "How the fuck they get them?"

Duke lowered his head. "They caught me and Shana slipping coming out of the Boys and Girls club. And apparently, they snatched up my daughter from Philly. I ain't asked how they wound up getting a hold of her because I fear the worst, but one thing is for sure you gotta help me get 'em back." Duke mugged him when he stopped and noticed Kammron was actually naked.

Kammron sighed and sat on the arm of the couch. "How the fuck you expect me to help you? I don't know where he holding them." Kammron got up and headed to his bedroom. He picked his boxers up off the floor and slipped them on. Shana was in the love seat nodding in and out. Every so often she would scratch herself.

"I'm finna get me a whole stable of young hoes. I'm finna draft these bitches from high school into the pros," he said out loud to nobody.

When he made it back into the hallway Duke was just going into the room where Kammron usually kept the money that was dropped off to him. "Say, nigga, where the fuck are you going?" Kammron yelled.

Duke rushed into the room. "Jason said he needs five million, Kammron. Come on man, I know we got it. I need that money so I can save my girls man." Duke's eyes were watery.

He could only imagine what Jason and his crew had in store for Deanna and Shana if he couldn't come up with the money. Duke opened the closet door and removed the wall inside of it. He knew it was where Kammron kept some of his safes that were usually stacked with cash. He thought he shoulda been able to come up with at least two million and some change. He had close to one million at his own home in a safe. He figured he would put what he had along with what he came up with from Kammron and get as close to five million as possible.

"Come on, Kammron, help me pull these safes out of here."

Kammron mugged him again. "Bruh, what the fuck is you talking about? I ain't said I was finna allow my money to get caught up in the middle of whatever is going on. That shit ain't got nothin' to do wit' me. Shana is yo' responsibility now, not the Kid's. Come on, get the fuck out of here." Kammron snapped his fingers and tried to lead Duke toward the hallway by his arm.

Duke yanked his arm away from Kammron. "Nigga, I ain't going nowhere until you give me this money. At the very least do it for, Deanna. She ain't got nothin' to do with none of this bullshit, she's just a kid."

Kammron sucked his teeth. "Duke you been out here getting money just like me. Nigga go holla at your stash, I ain't coming off my shit. Far as I'm concerned this ain't nothing but the spoils of war. The God don't negotiate with terrorists. Come on, get out of my shit."

Duke remained with his head down. His chest raised and fell in anger. He couldn't believe how selfish Kammron was being, at that moment wanted to take his life. He slowly trailed his eyes up until they were locked on the .40 Caliber that Kammron held.

"A'ight, B, that's how you gon' play shit? Cool then." He made it seem as if he was simply going to walk past him but as soon as he was close enough, he tackled him into the wall and slammed his hand against the edge of the doorway causing Kammron to drop the .40. It slid into the hallway just in front of the door. They rustled and tussled. They wound up on the floor wrestling with Duke on top. "I need that money, Kammron. Why the fuck are you taking me through all of this? We supposed to be brothers."

Kammron pumped his hips to toss Duke off him. He sat up and head-butted Duke. Duke flew backward. Kammron slid across the floor on his stomach. He was just about to grab ahold of the gun when Bonkers slammed his Timb on it. Kammron looked up and saw Bonkers with his arm around Henny's neck and a Glock aimed at him. The hallway was cluttered with masked men holding guns and machetes.

Bonkers curled his upper lip. "Am I my brother's keeper, Kammron?"

To Be Continued...
Coke Kings 4
Coming Soon

Submission Guideline

Submit the first three chapters of your completed manuscript to ldpsubmissions@gmail.com, subject line: Your book's title. The manuscript must be in a .doc file and sent as an attachment. Document should be in Times New Roman, double spaced and in size 12 font. Also, provide your synopsis and full contact information. If sending multiple submissions, they must each be in a separate email.

Have a story but no way to send it electronically? You can still submit to LDP/Ca$h Presents. Send in the first three chapters, written or typed, of your completed manuscript to:

LDP: Submissions Dept
Po Box 870494
Mesquite, Tx 75187

DO NOT send original manuscript. Must be a duplicate.

Provide your synopsis and a cover letter containing your full contact information.

Thanks for considering LDP and Ca$h Presents.

T.J. Edwards

BOW DOWN TO MY GANGSTA

By **Ca$h**

TORN BETWEEN TWO

By **Coffee**

BLOOD STAINS OF A SHOTTA **III**

By **Jamaica**

STEADY MOBBIN **III**

By **Marcellus Allen**

RENEGADE BOYS IV

By Meesha

BLOOD OF A BOSS **VI**

SHADOWS OF THE GAME II

By **Askari**

LOYAL TO THE GAME **IV**

LIFE OF SIN **III**

By **T.J. & Jelissa**

A DOPEBOY'S PRAYER **II**

By **Eddie "Wolf" Lee**

IF LOVING YOU IS WRONG... **III**

By **Jelissa**

TRUE SAVAGE **VII**

By **Chris Green**

BLAST FOR ME **III**

DUFFLE BAG CARTEL **IV**

HEARTLESS GOON **II**

By **Ghost**

A HUSTLER'S DECEIT III

KILL ZONE **II**

BAE BELONGS TO ME III

SOUL OF A MONSTER III

By **Aryanna**

THE COST OF LOYALTY **III**

By **Kweli**

A GANGSTER'S SYN III

By **J-Blunt**

KING OF NEW YORK V

RISE TO POWER III

COKE KINGS IV

BORN HEARTLESS II

By **T.J. Edwards**

GORILLAZ IN THE BAY IV

De'Kari

THE STREETS ARE CALLING II

Duquie Wilson

KINGPIN KILLAZ IV

STREET KINGS III

PAID IN BLOOD II

Hood Rich

SINS OF A HUSTLA II

ASAD

TRIGGADALE III

Elijah R. Freeman

MARRIED TO A BOSS III

By Destiny Skai & Chris Green

KINGZ OF THE GAME IV

Playa Ray

SLAUGHTER GANG III

RUTHLESS HEART

By Willie Slaughter

THE HEART OF A SAVAGE II

By Jibril Williams

FUK SHYT II

By Blakk Diamond

THE DOPEMAN'S BODYGAURD II

By Tranay Adams

TRAP GOD

By Troublesome

YAYO II

By S. Allen

GHOST MOB

Stilloan Robinson

KINGPIN DREAMS

By Paper Boi Rari

CREAM

By Yolanda Moore

Available Now

RESTRAINING ORDER **I & II**

By **CA$H & Coffee**

LOVE KNOWS NO BOUNDARIES **I II & III**

By **Coffee**

RAISED AS A GOON I, II, III & IV

BRED BY THE SLUMS I, II, III

BLAST FOR ME I & II

ROTTEN TO THE CORE I II III

A BRONX TALE I, II, III

DUFFEL BAG CARTEL I II III

HEARTLESS GOON

A SAVAGE DOPEBOY

HEARTLESS GOON

By **Ghost**

LAY IT DOWN **I & II**

LAST OF A DYING BREED

BLOOD STAINS OF A SHOTTA I & II

By **Jamaica**

LOYAL TO THE GAME

LOYAL TO THE GAME II

LOYAL TO THE GAME III

LIFE OF SIN I, II

By **TJ & Jelissa**

BLOODY COMMAS I & II

SKI MASK CARTEL I II & III

KING OF NEW YORK I II,III IV

T.J. Edwards

RISE TO POWER I II

COKE KINGS I II III

BORN HEARTLESS

By **T.J. Edwards**

IF LOVING HIM IS WRONG…I & II

LOVE ME EVEN WHEN IT HURTS I II III

By **Jelissa**

WHEN THE STREETS CLAP BACK I & II III

By **Jibril Williams**

A DISTINGUISHED THUG STOLE MY HEART I II & III

LOVE SHOULDN'T HURT I II III IV

RENEGADE BOYS I II III

By **Meesha**

A GANGSTER'S CODE I &, II III

A GANGSTER'S SYN II

By J-Blunt

PUSH IT TO THE LIMIT

By **Bre' Hayes**

BLOOD OF A BOSS **I, II, III, IV, V**

SHADOWS OF THE GAME

By **Askari**

THE STREETS BLEED MURDER **I, II & III**

THE HEART OF A GANGSTA I II& III

By **Jerry Jackson**

CUM FOR ME

CUM FOR ME 2

CUM FOR ME 3

CUM FOR ME 4

CUM FOR ME 5

An **LDP Erotica Collaboration**

BRIDE OF A HUSTLA **I II & II**

THE FETTI GIRLS **I, II& III**

CORRUPTED BY A GANGSTA I, II III, IV

BLINDED BY HIS LOVE

By **Destiny Skai**

WHEN A GOOD GIRL GOES BAD

By **Adrienne**

THE COST OF LOYALTY I II

By Kweli

A GANGSTER'S REVENGE **I II III & IV**

THE BOSS MAN'S DAUGHTERS

THE BOSS MAN'S DAUGHTERS II

THE BOSSMAN'S DAUGHTERS III

THE BOSSMAN'S DAUGHTERS IV

THE BOSS MAN'S DAUGHTERS **V**

A SAVAGE LOVE **I & II**

BAE BELONGS TO ME I II

A HUSTLER'S DECEIT I, II, III

WHAT BAD BITCHES DO I, II, III

SOUL OF A MONSTER I II

KILL ZONE

By **Aryanna**

A KINGPIN'S AMBITON

A KINGPIN'S AMBITION **II**

By **Qay Crockett**

TO DIE IN VAIN

SINS OF A HUSTLA

By **ASAD**

BROOKLYN HUSTLAZ

By **Boogsy Morina**

BROOKLYN ON LOCK I & II

By **Sonovia**

GANGSTA CITY

By **Teddy Duke**

A DRUG KING AND HIS DIAMOND I & II III

A DOPEMAN'S RICHES

HER MAN, MINE'S TOO I, II

CASH MONEY HO'S

By Nicole Goosby

TRAPHOUSE KING **I II & III**

KINGPIN KILLAZ I II III

STREET KINGS I II

PAID IN BLOOD

By **Hood Rich**

LIPSTICK KILLAH **I, II, III**

CRIME OF PASSION I & II

By **Mimi**

STEADY MOBBN' **I, II, III**

By **Marcellus Allen**

WHO SHOT YA **I, II, III**

Renta

T.J. Edwards

GORILLAZ IN THE BAY **I II III**

DE'KARI

TRIGGADALE I II

Elijah R. Freeman

GOD BLESS THE TRAPPERS I, II, III

THESE SCANDALOUS STREETS I, II, III

FEAR MY GANGSTA I, II, III

THESE STREETS DON'T LOVE NOBODY I, II

BURY ME A G I, II, III, IV, V

A GANGSTA'S EMPIRE I, II, III, IV

THE DOPEMAN'S BODYGAURD

Tranay Adams

THE STREETS ARE CALLING

Duquie Wilson

MARRIED TO A BOSS… I II

By Destiny Skai & Chris Green

KINGZ OF THE GAME I II III

Playa Ray

SLAUGHTER GANG I II

By Willie Slaughter

THE HEART OF A SAVAGE

By Jibril Williams

FUK SHYT

By Blakk Diamond

DON'T F#CK WITH MY HEART I II

By Linnea

ADDICTED TO THE DRAMA I II III

Coke Kings 3

By Jamila

YAYO

By S. Allen

BOOKS BY LDP'S CEO, CA$H

TRUST IN NO MAN

TRUST IN NO MAN 2

TRUST IN NO MAN 3

BONDED BY BLOOD

SHORTY GOT A THUG

THUGS CRY

THUGS CRY 2

THUGS CRY 3

TRUST NO BITCH

TRUST NO BITCH 2

TRUST NO BITCH 3

TIL MY CASKET DROPS

RESTRAINING ORDER

RESTRAINING ORDER 2

IN LOVE WITH A CONVICT

Coming Soon

BONDED BY BLOOD 2

BOW DOWN TO MY GANGSTA

Coke Kings 3

CPSIA information can be obtained
at www.ICGtesting.com
Printed in the USA
BVHW051739300623
666647BV00010B/342